T0165373

Ma Grandmere

At the Edge of Her Bed

Joel M. Mulholland

iUniverse, Inc.
New York   Bloomington

iUniverse books may be ordered through booksellers or by contacting:

iUniverse
1663 Liberty Drive
Bloomington, IN 47403
www.iuniverse.com
1-800-Authors (1-800-288-4677)

ISBN: 978-1-4401-8334-8 (sc)
ISBN: 978-1-4401-8335-5 (ebook)
ISBN: 978-1-4401-8337-9 (dj)

Printed in the United States of America

iUniverse rev. date:10/29/2009

Thanks dad for believing in me. Sound off the shofar in celebration!

This book is a result of my grandmother's life works fulfilled. She now belongs to the angels. While my father grand, as one with his lovely bride, I thank you for being a great strength in my life. Thank you for sharing with me your stories and personal thoughts of your generation.

And finally to the reader. Listen to the heart of the words and the soul of the scriptures.

Contents

Ma Grandmere
At The Edge of Her Bed
Written By
Joel M. Mulholland

Introduction

"Reflection is a flower of the mind, giving out wholesome fragrance."

Step outside of yourself and look at the family you have. Then take away a piece of that unity-the one that draws you all together. My grandpa, in his cowboy way, used a great example when he expressed it this way; "If you look at a wagon wheel, grandma is the hub, and the family members are the spokes." Our grandmother kept the wheel turning, keeping our family together with instruction and love.

The death of someone close to your heart leaves you with an overwhelming sense of void. Suddenly, life is taken, the body is lifeless, and the soul is gone. As a Christian, you struggle between knowing they are truly at peace, and where they want to be, and the natural, human selfishness of wanting to keep them with you. But it has taught me that with the sting of each death, comes new growth and maturity. You have to face life without those elders you leaned on, and didn't realize it.

Most of us were taught to respect and listen to our elders. Their instruction abides in our conscience. It guides us when needed and a greater appreciation of their life becomes a priority when they die. You realize how much you needed their love and how much was shared between you and your elders.

My grandma left us many treasures. Her spirit remains in these gifts. Perhaps, for that reason, I don't want to let her go. I want the world to know who she was! Years of letters, journal entries, endless personal writings and remembered fellowship with others will pull you in and give you complete understanding of her journey. Then the tributes from others and the impressions she left in their own lives give proof to her aspirations.

I know that her soul is with Jesus. That allows me to let go. Come, walk with me on a journey into the life of a woman of dignity, discipline, and the obedience of faith in the Lord. While showing her loyalty to her husband, children, and grandchildren. A woman with focused energy, and relentless commitment to her writing. Even up until her hand could write no more. A woman with the gift of giving to others without restraint or hesitation. Most importantly, she gave of herself freely in love through Christ Jesus. Not just mush, but true love. (A new commandment I give unto you, That ye love one another; as I have loved you, that ye also love one another.) John 13:34.

I wish to share with you her personal thoughts; genuine reflection, and the influence she had on others around her. She spoke the truth, the "two-edged sword," and knew it's correction and application in her own life. She presented it to others in love. She spoke the truth, and let the Holy Spirit apply it.

This about the reality that my grandma lived and shared with her family and friends. It's about a girl who grew up in God's word and chose to abide by it in her generation. It's about a girl who grew into a woman in Christ.

I believe the Word of God created a resilience in her spirit and body right up to her death. She knew that living in Jesus there is only death of the body not the soul. Grandma would often say, "We are kindred spirits Joel, no matter where we are."

This comforts me to this very day. Each piece of knowledge she has left me guides me along my way.

With each beginning, grandma insisted that I pray. So I prayed, "Lord give me strength and knowledge to write it as she would want it, and the way you would have it, always and Amen. Therefore, having done so, I give to you my grandmere."

Chapter 1
(Psalm 16:6 The lines are fallen unto me in pleasant places; yea, I have a goodly heritage)

With grandma, everything started with God! She saw God's Word in everything. So with joy I began with this letter.

15 January 2005,

(My dearest granddaughter, Joel. We must always start in the beginning: in the Hebrew, bereshit, meaning creation, in the Greek, meaning birth or origin. Our God always begins with the positive. So, In the beginning God created. (Genesis 1:1) Then in the gospel (John 1:1). In the beginning was the word and the word was with God, and the word was God. Said is word; to mention, calling attention to something. First we must believe God's word, or there's no point in going on.) Those are the words grandma wrote to me at the beginning of 2005.

So we must begin with our family history. When I think about my family history, I have a real sense of where I came from, and a real knowing of who each member was, not just pictures of people and the past. Grandma brought them to life for me. Describing their personality, occupations, and their relation to her, and I. Grandma always made it very clear, saying, "I feel you need to know where you came from, to know where you are going. For the old can inspire the new, which in turn can be left for the generations to come and shall be blessed by our father in heaven."

Darlene Mae Cory's family began across the Atlantic ocean. Her mother's Grandfather, Johann (John) Albert Munsterman, was born July 30, 1850 in Unzenberg, Germany. He later came to the United States and married Louise Jacobs. in Carroll, IA. Louise was born in Germany in 1856. Born to this union was a son named Johann W. Munsterman (John Jr.) born March 01, 1877 in Illinois and a daughter Lizzie Munsterman. John Jr. then married Maria Justice (Mary), in Jefferson Iowa, 1900. They had two daughters Frances and Daisy Frieda Anna Munsterman. (Daisy being my grandma's mother). Daisy was born on February19,1902. She was born in Coon Rapids, Carroll, Iowa. John, Daisy's father, died very young at the age of 28 of Brights Disease, in 1905. He left behind his wife Mary and two daughters. His widow Mary had no way to support her daughters. She began seeing a man named Earnest Donahue from Newton, Iowa. Earnest did not want kids. He told Mary she could come with him, but she couldn't bring her two daughters. Mary left Daisy and Frances behind and placed them in an orphanage.

Here is where the Munsterman and Cory families come together. Now remember John Munsterman, Daisy's birth father. His sister Lizzie married into the Cory family. She married Henry A. Cory. He being the son of William H. Cory. William came from England and married Louisa Stambaugh. They had ten children all together.

Lizzie told her husband Henry, "I can't abandon my niece Daisy and leave her in an orphanage when her sister Frances has already been adopted." So shortly after, Henry A. Cory and Lizzie (Munsterman) Cory took Daisy Munsterman and raised her as their own. They also made use of Daisy's small inheritance from her father. There is no documentation that they adopted Daisy.

Henry's brother, Thaddeus Lincoln Cory was born August 31, 1869 in Marion, IA. Thaddeus married Rosa Hilgenberg in Scranton, Greene, Iowa. In this union Rosa gave birth to George Willis Cory on October 25, 1897, in Willow, Greene, Iowa. Ok, Guess what George did? Yep, He married Daisy Munsterman, who was being raised by his uncle Henry and aunt Lizzie.

My grandmother wrote to me, "George Willis Cory and Daisy Frieda Munsterman were united in marriage on November 14, 1919, in Carroll, IA. Their wedding picture portrayed a beautiful couple. Grandma noted what the Coon Rapids Enterprise said in regards to her parents marriage. Volume 36-November 21, 1919. Munsterman-Cory married Friday. Miss Daisy Munsterman and George Cory were married last Friday at Carroll, IA. The bride is the daughter of John Munsterman, deceased, who died many years ago and who since her father's death has most of the time made her home with Henry Cory. She is by everyone spoken of as a most excellent young women. Of the groom, also commendable words can be said . He is an industrious young man and otherwise of good habits, and owns one of the dray lines and has a good business. He is the son of Thad and Rosa Cory. Friends heartily congratulate the newlyweds and wish them a full measure of happiness."

So my great grandmother Daisy Munsterman and great grandfather George Cory were married, and two years later, were blessed with the birth of Darlene Mae Cory.

My Grandma, Darlene Mae, at 82 wrote out her thoughts for me about her birth. On October23, 2004 she writes:

(Dear one Joel, dearest granddaughter. I will be praying the enclosed pages may give you a deeper insight, into your grandma Darlene's life and times, and how my times are in his hands [God's]. My heart is enlarged with love and praise as I contemplate, His way with me.)

This portion comes from:

"The Medical History of Darlene Mae Long."

"For thou hast possessed my reins. Thou hast covered me in my mother's womb. I will praise thee. For I am fearfully and wonderfully made; marvelous are thy works and that my soul knoweth right well. My substance was not hid from thee, when I was made in secret, and curiously wrought in the lowest parts of the earth. Thine eyes did see my substance, yet being imperfect; and in thy book all my members were written, which were fashioned when as yet there was none of them. How precious also are thy thoughts unto me- O God! How great are the sum of them!" (Psalm 139:13-17)

"Darlene Mae Cory was born, 'trailing clouds of glory' from God who is my home. I couldn't help thinking of that quotation by Wadsworth."

"I was born in the beautiful state of Iowa, on a farm in Greene county. The year was 1922. We read about the 'roaring twenties,' but I'm still not quite sure what the phrase meant. At that time it meant nothing to me."

Every child has a few medical ailments, and grandma had a few of her own.

"It was August 15th early in the evening, I've heard my mother recount, she was in the tomato patch picking tomatoes. Dr. Harvey was the man who attended to my mother at birth. He examined my mother and came to the conclusion that it would be a few hours. Soon after midnight, making it August 16th , I was born to George Willis and Daisy Anna Cory."

"The birth certificate records said it was a normal birth. Congenital hernia above the navel which was inherited from my father. While growing up in Coon Rapids, my family doctor was Dr. Channing. It was his opinion that the hernia would close in childhood."

"I was given enemas as a baby, and as a child. I used to sob for hours after these enemas (injection of water into the colon area). I would sob saying, 'Don't want no jection momma!' I remember this very vividly. I also couldn't tolerate cows milk, I was given Horlicks malted milk. Resulting in a plump healthy baby. I still can't tolerate cow's milk to this day. No shots given. I was a very healthy baby and child."

"In 1927, at age 5, I was scalded on my back with hot water at a neighbor's house. Then between 5 and 6, I stuck my tongue on a delicious, frozen pipe at Bowman's meat market. It tore all the skin off my tongue. My mother carried me dripping with blood all the way to the doctor's office. It was very uncomfortable for awhile."

"In 1930, I was 8 years old, a few childhood diseases were my lot. First there was Chicken Pox, then the measles followed. I rather enjoyed these afflictions because my dear mother made me very comfortable. Then I had a bout with Yellow jaundice, I was very sick. I never had any broken bones."

Grandma's childhood started off healthy and strong with the exception of the few illnesses many children encounter.

I remember that grandma dreaded to drink milk. She never cared for it unless she used it on hot or cold cereal. "Yuhk," she would say.

Between the age of 12 or 13 grandma was saved in Christ, and the next few events of her life would be the beginning of her close relationship with the Lord Jesus.

In closing this chapter, I give you a poem that she wrote. I found it in the front of one of the Bibles she sent to me. This Bible she was using when she was 17. The poem was hand written. It shows her faith in the Lord in her time of need, even as a young lady. A portrait of how God was beginning to mold her trust in him.

"When Jesus Whispers"
When the storm clouds gather and my spirit's low,

To my secret place of prayer I go.
There I listen for a voice so true,
I will not leave you comfortless,
I will come to you.
When from the darkness of tonight,
there came a blessed, holy light.
It was my Jesus and a cross he bare,
Then I saw too, this cross I must share.
When the way is long and the road is rough,
And your heart doth cry, "It is enough."
Lean hard on me and your strength renew,
For I will be here to comfort you.
So in sweet communion all my fears subside,
And my heart in him abides.
I realize then what it is to be,
consumed by love in Gethsemane.

Chapter 2
(Psalm 68:5 A father of the fatherless, and a judge of the widows, is God in his holy place.)

On January 7th, 1934, grandma was 12 years old and stepped out into the bitter, Iowa winter to go sledding. She recalls the events of this year.

"Year of trauma! It was cold and snowy, and the hill in front of Coder's funeral home was just right for sledding. I went out with some friends and took along my small sled. As I went down the hill a large toboggan came at me and surely would have smashed me if it hadn't been for Jay Churchill, who pushed me out of the way. I suffered a bruise on my right leg and a few scratches. My father showed great concern."

Grandma's father was a very handsome man, and grandma loved him very much. Every now and then she would pull out the old photo albums, and we would look at the pictures for hours just for fun. The photo albums had gold trim on the edge of the pages. Each album looked like a huge diary to me with a heavy metal latch on the side. You would never find anything so unique or of such quality today.

I remember when I was about 10, grandma and grandpa had just moved back from Pennsylvania. They were living with my aunt and uncle, Rose and Bob until they found a place again in Cedar Rapids, IA. They were staying in a room down in their basement. Grandma and I laid on the bed and reminisced, while looking through the albums. She would use her soft, story like voice and take me back to the roaring twenties. She did it so well, it was as if I were there. Grandma would describe the fashion, the vehicles, and the music of those days. I loved to hear her describe it all. The pictures were well preserved, and I loved to look at them. The color, texture, and style of the photos even intrigued me. The thought of a different life and time, other than my own fascinated me. Most of the pictures were in black and white and that forced you to use your imagination. It was exciting to me and I absorbed her words of the past like a sponge.

Her father always dressed very respectably. He looked very sharp, with a pressed shirt and bow tie. I would say almost a perfect face and beautiful eyes. Grandma writes of a darker side to him. She always carried this with her; we talked of it often, only she spoke of it in Jesus' name. When she spoke I could hear her yearning, to have her time with him-although cut to short.

"My father must have had these depressed thoughts, but one time in my father's life, he confessed Jesus as his savior and was baptized in the Christian church. On January 8th, 1934, my father was at work. He worked nights in the Armour's Creamery in Coon Rapids, Iowa. I was in bed. About ten or eleven o' clock some dear friends of ours came. It was the Waymires, Fred Mary and their children from Cooper, Iowa. Their son Nathaniel went down to the creamery, and there in the boiler room he found (my tragedy) my father, dead. A bullet through his heart."

"There has always been speculation and uncertainty behind this tragedy. The death certificate said the cause of death was a gunshot wound to the head. There was a business rivalry between my father's family, and the business of a family that was related because his mother belonged to that family. The business they were involved in was the dray business, (dray being: a vehicle used to haul goods, a strong low cart or wagon without sides), basically the hauling business. This business was very competitive. About two or three weeks before he was killed there was a fight between him and some of the other family at the train yards for a load to be carried. I have always left it to God as to what really took place."

This is where grandma's faith in Jesus began to be a part of her daily life right up to her death.

" Here is where the heavenly Father, our Father came to our rescue. This tragedy sent my mother and I into shock. I was not able to talk about it for a long time."

At 15 years old, Grandma's spiritual relationship with Jesus began to blossom.

She writes, " Hard times fell on mother and I, but we were happy. Mother worked hard at many jobs. The Lord heard many of our cries for help. He provided for our material and spiritual needs. We attended the Open Bible Church in Cooper, Iowa for awhile." (Proverbs 22:6) Train up a child in the way he should go; and when he is old, he will not depart from it. Note: The word train, in Hebrew, means: to narrow; to institute or discipline: dedicate. Parents are to consciously, actively institute religious training, and discipline their children according to God's word."

It was great grandma Daisy's own faith, as well as her example that took strong root in my grandma. My dad told me that grandma Daisy would buy a Bible, read it, fill it with personal notes, then would have underlining, underlining and more underlining, buy another one and start all over again. She knew her salvation was only through Christ Jesus. He has emphasized over and over how my grandmother's, mother was a huge anchor for her. My father spoke of grandma Daisy being very giving. This came from her own life experiences. She had a great appreciation for what she had.

In 1942 great grandma Daisy married Frank Kirk. Much later in grandma's life her mother gave her a prayer. It gives you a sense of how great grandma felt about life and wanted her own daughter to see that as well.

16 August 1976

"A Prayer"

Let me do my work each day and if the darkened hours of despair overcome me, may I not forget the strength that comforted me in the desolation of other times. May I still remember the bright hours that found me walking over the silent hills of my childhood, or dreaming on the margin of the quiet river, when a light glowed within me, and I promised my early God to have courage amid the tempests of the changing years. Spare me from bitterness and from the sharp passions of unguarded moments! May I not forget that purity and riches are of the spirit. Though the world know me not, may my thoughts and actions be such as shall keep me friendly with myself. Lift my eyes from the earth, and let me not forget the uses of the Stars. Forbid that I should judge others lest I condemn myself. Let me not follow the clamor of the world, but walk calmly in my path. Give me a few friends who will love me for what I am; and keep ever burning before my vagrant steps the kingly light of hope. And though age and infirmity overtake me, and I come not within sight of the castle of my dreams, teach me still to be thankful for life, and for time's olden memories that are good and sweet: and may the evenings twilight find me gentle still.

Love,
Mother (Daisy A. Kirk)

The Heavenly Father became my grandma's true father. Moreover, I emphasize her mother was a strong influence in her relationship with Jesus, especially after her father passed away. It is very apparent in these two poems she wrote when she was 15. She was growing in her spirit, and letting God begin to heal and bless her:

"Be Ye Separate"
"Come out," I heard my Savior calling,
His voice so sweet and clear.
"Come out," in my ear it was ringing,
And I will take away all fear.
His love so great and fine,
My heart longed to receive.
"Come out, thou shalt be mine"
His voice, I could believe.
I considered for awhile,
The price so small, and yet so great.
Lo, I saw the Savior smile
And say, "Be ye separate."
I've come out and I'm so happy
That I'm a child of God,
And I know that he will help me,
Though I pass beneath the rod.
Darlene Mae Cory

Grandma reveals, "I was a happy teen in spite of hard times. From 1938 to 1943 my focus was on high school. Books, teachers, friends, girls and boys. I dated several different ones. I had a good figure, attractive- if I do say so. Glad to be alive. A faith and trust in God, and my Savior who had brought me thus far."

"In 1940 I graduated from high school in Coon Rapids. I had a deeper desire to go on to college, but I didn't see how it could be financed. Then my mother and I began to attend the Free Methodist Church. Here is where my experience in

Jesus deepened. I attended revivals with brother Ballenger and Kendall. It was a beautiful time in my life. I even declined to go to my junior/senior banquet one year because a revival was on at the Free Methodist church I was attending."

Her teenage years draw to a close and grandma now has the foundation that begins to shape her future in the Lord. As a young Christian, grandma noted in her Bible: Therefore if any man be in Christ, he is a new creature: old things are passed away behold, all things are become new. (2 Cor. 5:17)

She writes, "We are born into sin, but the spirit giveth life. The carnal mind becomes dead, renewed and alive in Christ."

Chapter 3
(Song of Solomon 1:2(Let him kiss me with the kisses of his mouth: for thy love is better than wine.)

I am truly blessed to have had a grandmother who wrote all her life. In her 70's, she wrote out her journey with her husband. I am so thankful. I would have never known any of these events if she hadn't passed them along to me.

She begins as always with the Word of God: (Psalms 119:54) Thy statutes have been my songs in the house of my pilgrimage. From her special writing, she entreats us with how her relationship with her husband began.

"Songs In The House Of Our Pilgrimage"

"Gerald and Darlene were blessed at an early age to hear and know the joyful sound, the good news that Jesus loved us and called us to repent and walk in the light of his countenance."

"We met in a quaint and beautiful old Free Methodist church in 1935, in Coon Rapids, Iowa. We were 13 at the time. My mother and I lived across the street from the church. Gerald, his mother, father, brother and sister attended the church as well. I dated both Gerald and his brother Roy. Gerald and I were friends as teenagers and were a part of the youth group. He teased me and pulled my hair, incessantly. I guess because he liked me. There was a lady pastor, a sister Brown, and she took a deep interest and concern in nurturing our faith and providing clean, youthful gatherings for us. When I was 15, I rode with sister Brown in her Model T Ford to Boone, Iowa to a district meeting. Gerald came with his parents, and we began to notice each other. We shared spiritual experiences as we responded to the conviction of the Word of God. Both of us knew God had called us to give our life to him."

"The next few years, the music played different melodies. Gerald went to Guthrie Center high school and was involved in football. I had other interests. He had to stay out for a year and help his father on the farm, he graduated in 1942."

"Gerald left for Central College in Kansas, he stayed for one semester. The Japanese had bombed Pearl Harbor, so Gerald decided to enlist in the army because he thought he would be drafted."

"After graduation I was working in two local restaurants and a clothing store."

"My mother and I always found our refuge and hope in God's Word. There were times when my walk was not steady and steadfast, but God is so faithful, restoring my soul."

"Meanwhile I was dating a young man by the name of Jerry Gettler. Jerry was in the Navy, and before he left he gave me an engagement ring. While waiting for him I was working in the North Side Café, owned by George Boehler. That's when Gerald had come back from college and enlisted in the army."

"When he got back he came into the Café and we talked, being friends, and that night he persuaded me to let him take me home. He persuaded me we belonged together. As a result of my prayers, I broke my engagement to Jerry. He was of the Catholic faith and his father was very angry with me. But as I prayed I didn't feel led to continue in the engagement with Jerry. I guess the Spirit's leading brought Gerald and I together."

"The music began again. We attended a camp meeting early in 1943. Gerald rededicated his life to Jesus, and I knew God was my only refuge. We were both moved by natural and spiritual longings in the Lord. He proposed to me in the Coon Rapids Park to a band stand, and I said, 'Yes,' and so it was, August 27th, 1943 we were married in the Free Methodist church in Boone, Iowa. The Reverend Biggerstaff officiating with the preacher's son standing up with Gerald, and Katherine Fowler standing with me."

"There was a wedding supper for us at the preacher's parsonage. My mother Daisy, Gerald's mother and father, William and Wilma Long. A few other friends were present as well. Very beautiful and pleasant. Wedding photos taken. Neither of us having much money. Gerald wore a brown suit, and I wore my newest suit. I received my suit at a reduced price because I worked for the Bower and Bower department store in Coon Rapids. I looked pert and sweet in my black, silk suit with cranberry colored sequins and a bouquet of roses."

"We returned to Coon Rapids where we spent our wedding night in the home of Mrs. Bertch Frolich. The room and everything else was very pleasant. I had a new, beautiful, peach colored nightdress. Then the next morning we left at 4 a.m. on the train for Sioux City, Iowa, where we spent our honeymoon at the Free Methodist parsonage, at the invitation of the parsonage family. There was a district church meeting there in a tent with Frank Dawson preaching. It was all very meaningful for us."

"We met the Robard family from Michigan at this time. They were a true blessing to us."

Grandma then says, "Joel, this was a very uncertain time, back in 1943. Our generation had come through the depression of the 30's and in 1932, when we were 10, there was high unemployment and a need for leadership. Franklin Delano Roosevelt won in the race for the presidency. The 'New Deal' was his brain child. Roosevelt picked up the pieces of the depression from where Hoover left off, as Hoover's administration didn't do much through the government to help the people. Roosevelt's administration created new jobs and the government helped the people get back on their feet."

Grandma continues, "There was an air of pause in living, like a melody, when there is a pause to savor the beauty of the song."

"After a couple of weeks or so together, Gerald left from the train station in Guthrie Center bound for Des Moines where the army of the U.S.A. claimed him the first week in October, 1943. Leaving me, his new bride behind. Mother and I had an apartment together. She was married to Frank, but he was in Galveston, Texas, in the army as well. So we were alone, both working and sharing expenses. I even sent Gerald money in Muskogee, OK while at camp Gruber. I worked from September to November at Coon Rapids Hybrid Seed Corn Co. owned by Garst & Thomas Hybrid Seed, known all over. I received a good paycheck, sorting Hybrid seed corn. My mom, Daisy worked there too."

Grandma opened up to me more than I expected as she continued to reveal to me her feelings in regards to her tall handsome military groom. " I wrote to Gerald and you read one or two of my letters. Joel, I missed him."

Grandma sent me one letter, and a poem that she had written to grandpa while he was in training in Muskogee. You can sense her loneliness while they were apart.

Grandma notes. Twelve days after we were married.

12 September 1943

(My dearest, There's so many things I want to say. I'm not just sure where to begin. First of all though, honey, I love you and miss you terribly. I never realized how much you've come to mean to me. Thursday afternoon the reality of your being gone struck me and I had a good cry, but I prayed and I'm better now.

Your suitcase came back this morning and I put all the papers away for safe keeping. Your folks or should I say 'the folks' were at church this morning and I told them you called and sent two cards and your suitcase home. They were all going out to Grandma Long's house or Sadie Drakes place today for dinner and wanted me to go, but I wanted to spend this afternoon writing you and resting, so I didn't go. I asked mom if she minded and she said no, but she felt I belonged to her part of the time now. That was so sweet, and I sure love your mom, honey.

Say the studio where you had your picture taken, darling, notified me that I could get one for a $1.95 or three for $5.00. I'd love to have one, but I haven't worked a week on the corn yet honey. I still have the $10.00 for our wedding pictures, I'm so disappointed about not getting them. I have to pay half of the rent this month and I wanted to send you a little if you needed it real bad. We'll only have Tues, Wed., Thurs., pay this week because the cut off is on Thurs. So I won't have much left this week, by the time I pay rent, eat, and send you a little. I want the picture so though, terribly. I wrote about our wedding pictures, do you suppose the proofs got lost or something? My imaginations running wild.

Roy and Helen said, 'hi' and for you to write.Honey, yesterday, all day, I felt so afraid and nervous. Afraid we'd made a mistake. Then last night when you called, I knew I loved you and it didn't make a difference what anyone else thought or said. I hope my darling that you feel the same. Roy was telling me, Thursday afternoon how you'd bought Kathryn a fur coat and how surprised they were when we were married. Several people have told me they were surprised when they heard I married you. I just try to let these things go in one ear and out the other. I am up at sister Gill's writing this, she's lying down and I'm here alone. Alone, that's a dreadful word. I wish you

17

were here for a big kiss, right now, honestly sweetheart, I'm starved. Ho! You will write me a big, long letter soon, won't you? And keep writing. Tomorrow, Monday, I'm going to work at Bowers. Tuesday I start on the corn, from 5 0' clock in the morning till 2 in the afternoon. Eight hour shifts, 1 hour off for lunch. I'll get your suit cleaned, your shoes half-soled, wash and iron your shirts and put them away. Have you been reading your testament honey? You aren't smoking! I hope. Oh, Gerald I love you so very much, please don't change from the way you were the day we got married.

You know something, a little pain went through my heart when I looked in your shirt pocket and found the poem I'd written to you, still in there. You were in a hurry I know and just forgot it. I meant it darling, so here it is again....

I love you darling, never fear,
And want you always to keep me near.
Your heart that's true and yielded to God
All down the future path we trod.
Let's work and play and love together,
In sunshine or in stormy weather.
Putting our lives into the hands of him,
Who saved us and made us whole within.
As you are about to leave me sweet,
I know life now, will be incomplete.
But each night dear, as I kneel in prayer,
I'll clasp your hand and meet you there.
Someday dear, the skies will be blue,
We'll bravely start our life anew.
With faith in God our life will be blessed,
He'll give us life, peace and rest.

Your Wife,
Darlene.

Your wife, it's so strange and new; it makes me feel queer, but I am yours darling, always, unless you change your mind. Forgive me if I've been a little musky in spots, but I am so lonesome for you today. I feel better when I'm working.

How come hon, you write Mrs. Darlene Long? Why not Mrs. Gerald Long? I just wondered why.

Well my dearest husband,

I've got to bring this manuscript to a finish here, I got going and couldn't stop. Write me almost every day, if you can.

All my love and kisses,
Darlene

P.S. This was inevitable, You haven't told me you loved me in four days. I guess the honeymoon's over. I love you. Really!! Forgive this crazy mood, I don't have them often. God bless you darling and keep you always)

On the envelope of this letter grandma writes to me, 60 years later in 2003, Joel, my heart at this time in 1943. After 60 years, yes! It must still linger, sweetly, in Jesus. He's seen us through it all. To my sometimes you give me that "I want to kick you in the butt feeling, but lets not dwell on that!

I can sense the uncertainty of the times. It reminded me of when I was first married and the newness of it all. I recall writing a lot of poems to my husband as well, very heart felt. There's a new found freedom in their relationship together. Just as their journey began, grandpa was called off to war along with the other millions of young soldiers who were separated from their brides at that time. Still it must have been an exciting time indeed.

Grandma was a new bride, without her husband, and you can feel the loneliness in her poems. Not withstanding, I can hear the anticipation of their reunion at last!

This next poem was written on grandpa's birthday, October 5, 1943 while he was at camp Gruber.

"To One who means the world to Me"

There is a room within my heart,
Pink and blue and set apart.
And bright and glorious with dreams come true,
That came to me when I found you.
When all outside is noise and din,
I steal away to this room within.
There mid the silence that love will impel,
I sense your presence and all is well.
Tis not a room of wood or stone,
But molded of love that's your very own.
So in the silence of our heart,
We are so near though far apart.

Your Wife,
Darlene Mae Long

"A very Happy Birthday again darling!"

"I longed to be with your grandfather, so I continued to work to save up enough money to go and be with him. In November, 1943, mother and I decided to go be with our husbands, Frank Kirk who mother had married in 1942 is in Galveston, and I to go be with Gerald in Muskogee, at Camp Gruber. I had enough money to go on the bus and be with my soldier husband."

Grandma paints this picture for me of the reunion in Muskogee.

"Life at 21 is exciting and a new adventure for me. I remember right now, at 82, the long bus ride, the soldiers, sailors and civilians filling the bus. The moon was full on the plain, and Joel, a deep orange journey seemed endless. Young, attired in a tan wrap around coat, pert white tam [a woolen cap of Scottish origin] and white boots, I was eager to be reunited with my soldier husband. Yet pleased at admiring glances from soldiers and sailors."

"Then at the bus station in Muskogee, how romantic to be a part of the tenderness of the times, seeing Gerald coming toward me in his uniform, tall, strong and handsome. Looking just as the picture I gave you, portrays. We, Gerald and I being a little past 21, it was romantic and exciting in 1943, being in the military atmosphere. Gerald and I were alone on the weekends, in a room I procured at 508 Irving Street, in Muskogee, Oklahoma. It was our first home. Mr. & Mrs. David Wadley, an older couple rented us this comfortable room, and I had kitchen privileges."

"I met good friends there. I met a staff sergeants wife, Betty Weisenborn. We became good friends and spent a lot of time together. While Gerald was at camp I worked and volunteered my service at a clinic ministering to the Indian children. The Lord comforted me when I had to be alone and his word has always nurtured my soul."

"I recall in December, 1943, at our apartment, Gerald was home and I became pregnant. In January of 1944 I realized a new little note was sounding within me. In late January, my mother came and took me back home to Coon Rapids, Iowa. Gerald was hearing rumors of going overseas. Soon his company 232, Field Artillery Battalion, A Battery-42nd infantry, Rainbow division was preparing to do just that."

"So, my mother, bless her, took care of me (her baby, having a baby). Anyway, months passed and on September 6, 1944, your first uncle was born. He was born in Jefferson, Iowa. Gerald didn't get to come home when he was born, they were on special maneuvers. He did come home when David was two weeks old for a bit. Then he had to leave to get ready to embark on his duty overseas. So my first born grew, and I was a lonely war bride. The Lord comforted and helped me while we were apart. He kept us. Praise his name!"

"In January, 1945, grandpa was first stationed in Marseille, France, and later sent northward into Germany."

"General Patton and the 3rd army were on their right. Grandpa and his battalion were camped on a hill side in Germany when president Roosevelt died. Grandpa remembers the thought of all the soldiers on the front, "Glad it wasn't a General or Major Collins. It was hard to replace a good general.""

Grandpa was with the 42nd Rainbow division, 232nd field artillery, battalion. I asked him how he felt being separated from his bride. He said, "I felt starved without her." Grandpa had his own thoughts on the war.

"My feelings about the war? The saying was from WW1, This is the war to end all wars, but this war will! When the war ended I was somewhere in Schweinfurt, Germany. At the end of my tour I was sent to Salzburg, Austria and flown home. It was based on a point system as to when you went home (time put in and other factors). I flew into New York City then road a train to Camp Kilmer in Illinois. There I received my discharge from the army. Then I road the train to Des Moines, Iowa. When I arrived in Des Moines I took a cab to the bus station and there your grandmother was waiting."

Again I asked, "Is there a lesson you learned from the war?"

Grandpa is silent for a moment. Then in his deep, firm voice he says, "The lesson I learned from the war? Discipline! The importance of enforcement! Sometimes that's just the way it has to be done! True instruction has to be maintained to get the job done. There were thousands lost and buried on foreign soil and yet, still no peace to this day. The peace just doesn't always follow up."

I asked grandpa if he felt a sense of accomplishment when he returned home. He stated, "I just wanted to go home!"

Grandpa's feeling when he came home and saw grandma in the station? "It was the same as when I saw her walking down the aisle at our 50th anniversary ceremony. It was a fervent feeling; a deep sincere emotion."

"When I opened the door to the station grandma was sitting at the end of the building, when she saw me, it seemed as if she jumped until she landed in my arms. The distance seemed longer than what it was, but at last I was reunited with my lovely bride!"

"Grandpa, what message do you have to your grandchildren and great grandchildren in regards to the war?"

He sighs heavily and says, "I'm sorry that we didn't do a good enough job the first time, in order for there to be peace, so you wouldn't have to live in turmoil and unrest now. But! There's never going to peace as long as there is evil. Until Jesus returns, there will continue to be wars."

In 2006 grandpa related to me his love for his beautiful bride, was often unspoken, but still extremely deep and fervent.

Grandma continues "There were adjustments when Gerald came home in 1945. There were different jobs for him in the town and on the farm, and between 1944 and 1958, I gave birth to 7 children."

"God reminded us of our commitment, and we were attending the church in Coon Rapids. Our first born was baptized by the Superintendent of the Iowa Conference. Then Bill came along, my spring time baby and a little crescendo in our lives in 1947. Gerald chose to become Coon Rapids night watchman."

"Later in 1947, we made the decision to move to Cedar Rapids, Iowa. My mother and step father lived there. My mother was attending (G) Ave Free Methodist Church." and was active in the services. We decided to attend there. The pastor was Carl Oleson."

"Then our Daniel (A sweet note and later my Jewish son) made up the trio in 1949. We were more faithful at church, but discordant notes were hovering."

"Then came Stephen, a quiet harmony. He made up our quartet in late 1950."

" Four years, busy with cares of this life. We loved God, but weren't faithfully serving him."

"Rosemary our little joy-bell came in 1954. Pink and beautiful, our first daughter."

"Praise God. Rebecca Ann, our little star, blessed us in 1956 on the first day of spring."

"Then Benjamin, strong, handsome, son of our right hand came in 1958."

"How we thanked God for all these blessings." "Gerald was employed at Iowa Steel when we first moved to Cedar Rapids. He was laid off from there after the military contract had run out for the company. The war was starting to wind down. He worked for 14 months there. Then around May of 1952, he began working for Penick and Ford LTD in Cedar Rapids (a corn processing company to produce starch for certain products to be made, like paper)."

"All these years a good husband and father, working steadily. With help from inheritances from both our families, we were able to purchase our first home in Cedar Rapids when our youngest was two. God was good to us and merciful. "

Chapter 4
(Proverbs 31:27-28 She looketh well to the ways of her household, and eateth not the bread of idleness. Her children arise up and call her blessed; her husband also, and he praiseth her)

My grandmother loved her children. She exemplified duty to home and family. Unmatched in my eyes! She speaks of her duty to them. Always in her prayers.

"Our children, raised in the church, most of the time at Free Methodist on G avenue. God intervening in my life to stay close to the church, and God moved in each child when they were young, attending Sunday school and church. We had family worship, but Gerald wasn't always there, working of course. In 1968, children all growing, from ages 24 down to 6 years. Occupied with their needs. Physically, spiritually, and emotionally. Forgive my mistakes, dear ones."

A true, mother's love for her children never ends, and mothering continues through the child's life. It doesn't matter if they are 5 or 45, endless guidance prevails in a mother's heart even when her children are no longer there.

I asked my grandmother to give me her thoughts on each one in March of 2004. Little did I know what was in store for me. First a few lines grandma underlined in a sweet book she sent to me.

"If you let your children grow without trimming their buds, don't expect many blossoms."

Grandma notes: "So true".

"A mother's patience is like a tube of toothpaste- It's never quite all gone."

My grandmother had a sweet sense of humor!

I received these words from my grandma, not long after my request for her thoughts. I was truly blessed by every word. She begins with a few words to me. Keep in mind "words" were a great part of grandma's life, and she would meticulously dissect every aspect of its meaning to better understand and learn.

March 26th, 2004:

"Beloved Joel and so much more! Before I give my hand to write, my heart asks for enrichment from the Holy Ghost in all my utterance, that it will please and glorify our Father God, in his precious Son Jesus. Our talk today, blessed me so. It came as I was waiting. You named a project. That is an interesting word, has varied meanings: 1. A definitely, formulated piece of research.2. Cast forward. 3. Present for consideration! 4. A beam of light. So, I present for consideration, some thoughts concerning my children."

Psalm 127:3, And lo children are an heritage of the Lord; and the fruit of the womb is his reward.

"I love my rewards", she says. Then grandma takes me back a bit.

"These first words are from 1968. Your oldest uncle D then (24), Bill (21), Dan (19), Stephen (18), Rose (14), Becky (12), Ben (10)."

"Now remember Joel, this was written in 1968, I was 46 years old. I wrote a letter to my beloved womb. I spoke of , at 22, my womb receiving a new beginning, and how it nourished and cared for this bundle of life until it's required time."

"My first born, beautiful, strong and healthy. I prayed each day of our life while he was growing in the womb, your wonderful warmth. His first cry seemed to waken all the other little miracles and my heart said, he will be a leader. Now a leader, a wonderful son and a good man. I prayed each day I carried him in your warm nest (my womb), that he would be strong in mind and body."

"God saw fit for my womb to house and nourish this son, William George, May 15, 1947. You covered him so wonderfully. A happy, healthy little fellow 8lbs., 6oz. Thank you dear womb for cherishing him so faithfully. Today, 21, he will carry the word of God to others. Bless his ministry dear God."

"The next time, you gave sustenance to Daniel. Just 19 years ago, dear womb, July 29, 1949. We were very busy helping Daniel come into the world. He, Daniel, a sensitive and intelligent young man. I know he will come through in your plan and design for his life. Bless him dear God. Guide and direct his steps."

"Then, dear first home of precious life, you were visited with another seed of life to nourish and develop. To give special calm and care. This was Stephen Joel. You did well with him. He was a big baby, 9lbs., 5oz., born on a November day, the 8th , 1950. He has grown so tall with a peaceful, determined spirit. I know he will find and achieve his goal. He is 18 now, dear womb, his first home, your quiet warmness."

"There were two times dear womb, when in God's wisdom, you saw fit to cease to nourish two embryos. Perhaps you were tired and not able, and God knew this in his wisdom. They are in his care, and growing , I believe."

"Then, March 4, 1954, came our darling, pink and white baby daughter. After four sons, you outdid and excelled in preparing us a beautiful daughter. We called her Rose Mary, for remembrance. God's goodness in remembering and giving us a daughter with pink and white skin as well as beautiful blue eyes. We spoiled her, dear womb, but it didn't hurt, because now at fourteen she is ready, always to do things for others. She is a wonderful cook. She is a beautiful and intelligent girl, who loves to read. God help her achieve her goals. Give her patience at just the right moment, then give her courage and open the way for her to do what she has in her heart to do. We are close, heart to heart."

"Then dear womb, on a beautiful first day of spring (a yellow, joyful day) March 21st, 1956, you gave us another grand production. Another little girl. What a blessing! Rebecca Ann seemed to be just the music for her name. Becky is your girl, dear God. She has heard your voice in her own little way. Perhaps you formed her, in our dear womb, dear God , to be thy servant. Watch over her. She has a brilliant mind, keep it ignited and feasting on thy truths. Help her to be patient, endure and walk in the path you have shown her. Thank you for her kindred spirit. "Well dear nourisher of life, once more you have housed and cared for a 'sweet' beginning." On August 13, 1958, he, Benjamin Phillip, stayed within you many days and weighed 9lbs and 12ozs when he was born. Dr Hayes was astounded at his size and you to had some difficulty helping him be born, also the Lord helping. Perhaps dear womb you were tired from long months of sustaining life, and perhaps you were injured during this time. But everything turned out fine and happy. Today Benjamin is strong at 10 years and is a good student. He wants to be a professional athlete and is working even now to realize his dream. Keep him, guide him dear God in your will for Benjamin Phillip."

"Let all my children, and grandchildren too, come trust in thee, O God. Be to them a personal God. The eternal God is our refuge and underneath are the everlasting arms, Jesus Christ."

"In my 40's, grandchildren coming. A little arthritis in my neck and feet. All through the 70's I was pretty healthy, very few colds and no flu."

"July 2, 1970 Darlene Mae Long, age 48."

Again grandma is praying for each of her children in Christ's name.

"What shall I do with the rest of my life? It is this day, I am alive. Thank God. Let everything that hath breath praise the Lord! I am thankful I am aware of who is my benefactor, my Savior, my life. Bless my husband, Oh God, this day, cause him to be aware of the angel of thy presence."

"O Jehovah, provide my son Bill with all his needs according to thy riches in glory. Help us, Gerald and I, to communicate with them. There is to be a grandchild. Bless it's development in Kendra's womb. I plead the blood of Jesus for this new life, cover it, Lord bless it, and give Kendra strength of body and peace of mind through confinement and delivery. Give Bill an unction from the Holy Spirit, O God, lead him on in thy truth. Make him a 'Good Shepherd.' I plead the blood just now for Bill, incline his heart, this day with love for his God, his wife, and his family. My heart cries out for Dan, O Lord, he is 21. You know him. You have spoken to him. He seems to have a (built in receiver) that receives the light, radiating from thy word. Holy Spirit of God, Dan aspires to draw closer to thee. Sometimes his fleshly lusts draw him away. Put a wall of fire about him, rescue him O God. Use him as you see fit. Keep that "hunger" in his heart and mind for that something beautiful that will "blossom" in his soul. I plead the blood of Jesus for Daniel. Thank you Lord for hearing prayer. I see him now, thy prophet, preaching truth everywhere with no reservations. Let it be so, O God, and if his drums and music are so much a part of him, let them herald the truth of thy coming. Amen, Lord. Oh Lord for our grandchild when it comes, love it already."

God answered that prayer. This shows the blessed hope of parent's prayers for their children. As Jesus said, If you shall ask anything in my name I will do it. (John 14:14)

Two years later God answered that prayer for her son as you can see by his own testimony.

Dad writes in the spirit,

"Doing drugs, music, and drinking…I was in hell, trying to find a heaven. But Jesus the Christ is the only way to heaven. Whether sins of the flesh or unbelief, without Jesus there's no way to heaven.

"I was doing my way without Jesus, and did ten days in jail.

"Sometime later, I realized I was separated from God, lost; that's why Christians ask you if you are saved. I was messed up and on my way to hell; Even if I hadn't done all those sinful things.

"One night I was sitting at my kitchen table, alone reading the Bible. The kitchen light was on, but suddenly a darkness came over my eyes. I couldn't see. No, it wasn't a black out, because even then you can see.

"Without thinking about it, I got on my knees at the chair, and cried out: "O God! Don't leave me this way!" And my sight returned.

"I was scared. I had to talk to someone. At that time my mother was already saved. She knew the Lord Jesus as her Savior and Lord. I knew it would be good to talk to her.

"I drove to my parent's house. It was 3 a.m. When I arrived, there was a light on in the kitchen. I walked to the front door and looked in the window. There at the kitchen table, sat my mother, with her head down on her Bible. When God does something, it all falls into place. I walked in and said: "Mom can we pray?

"We prayed together that morning in September 1972. I asked God to forgive me for my sins, and I asked Jesus to come into my heart.

"Jesus died on the cross to save everyone from sin, unbelief and the sins they have committed. His precious blood, shed for you and for me, is the only thing God will accept to wash away our sins.

"I went down on my knees, lost and afraid, and came up saved and celebrating.

"I know I'm saved! Jesus the Christ is my Savior and Lord. Jesus is the son of God.

He that has the Son has life; and he that has not the Son of God has not life. (1 John 5:12).

"I know that Jesus is the Christ. He is the Son of God. I know that God has forgiven me for lying, stealing, doing drugs, sex before marriage, adultery, and backsliding to name just a few."

If we confess our sins, (to God) he is faithful and just to forgive us our sins, and to cleanse us from unrighteousness. (1 John 1:19)

My father, now ministers wherever he is needed in the city of Cedar Rapids, IA. His salvation is a result of prayers stored in heaven and the example grandma set for him. It has brought light into my own life. The faithfulness she has instilled in dad has also been applied by him in my life and others.

When my dad and mom were married grandma made a family scrap book. After they divorced I kept the book. In it I found a piece where she is overjoyed with her children's new way of life.

"Dan born again, Thank you Jesus. Dan's verse when the Lord came and made him new, Praise God!" Come up in the morning and present thyself unto me in the top of the mount. (Exodus 34:2)

Her prayer and trust in Jesus brought my dad salvation.

"Then Sheryl, Lord Jesus Christ, Sheryl found Jesus, precious to her soul!"

Grandma rejoices in my mother being saved with this scripture:

That their hearts might be comforted, being knit together in love, and unto all riches of the full assurance of understanding, to the acknowledgement of the mystery of God, and of the Father, and of Christ; In whom are hid all the treasures of wisdom and knowledge. (Colossians 2:2-3).

"Then Lord, my son Stephen. You know where he is Lord, wearing the uniform of our land. God, you are with this lad. I know, you gave me this promise, speak comfort to his soul, spirit and mind. I plead the blood of Jesus for my Stephen. Give him the intellect and ability to pass these tests in this school (for military police.) Lead him Lord and strengthen. Let the angel of your presence be continually with him. Protect and cover him Lord with thy precious Spirit.

"Remember, Oh Lord, Marty, bless her heart with contentment. Help her to encourage him, and him to send her letters of hope and comfort. I plead the blood of Jesus for them. Lord keep them in thy hand."

"Holy spirit of God, move and hover over my daughter Rose Mary. Speak to her out of thy word. She is 16 years old, but she knows your word. Grant , Oh Lord, her hearts desire and may it be that which pleases thee."

"In her relationships, bless and keep her. Let not her heart be set on one person or thing. You have many wonderful things in store for her, I know. I plead the precious, holy blood of Jesus for her soul and body just now. Give her this day July 2,1970, a new purpose. Take away the boredom out of her heart and mind and give her creative thoughts. Oh God grant this prayer for Rose. Oh God, I tarry in thy presence. Jesus' blood is my only plea. A plea thy ear cannot turn away from." "Remember, Oh Lord, my daughter Rebecca. Her heart belongs to thee. Her whole life, I have seen at 14 years old, changes in her, Lord.

Thank you for speaking again to her heart and mind. Satisfy her heart and mind; Satisfy her heart with good things, from thee I plead the blood of Jesus for Becky. Use her in your vineyard. Help her to find her place to serve thee, that she will know you are with her and blessing her life. Keep her, Oh God, put a wall of fire of your holy spirit about her that will quench the fiery darts of the devil. Oh Lord, in Christ Jesus."

"And dear God, keep thy mighty hand on my son, 12 year old Benjamin. He belongs to you Oh Lord. He has many hopes and dreams to play in the world of sports. If that is thy will, grant him a healthy, strong body and an alert mind. May he use the material gain to glorify thee. Keep thy hand over him. I plead the blood of Jesus for my son. My youngest son Benjamin, thank you for giving him to me."

"Now Lord, the heat is upon me, and there are duties before me. Give me a heart attuned to thy will."

Grandma prayed often for her children, and the result was the true blessing and rewards she got from each of her children.

She continues with her thoughts. "Praise God, he brought us through. We saw all our children graduate; college for four of them, and now we started to see marriages and grandchildren. So blessed."

Late in 2007, I asked grandpa if anything stood out in his memory about my aunt and uncles from their childhood. He said this: "Well if you want to add a little humor to this writing of yours, I do recall a time when I came home from work and your father, Dan, and your uncle Steve were acting up; and were in trouble with their mother, and she was crying. I asked her what was wrong, and she said out of frustration: " I have given them a good swat and neither of them have cried."

Grandpa chuckled and said: "It was then we discovered they both had stuck a book in their britches."

Good try!

"Then there was one other time when we were in Killian's department store, downtown. I'm not sure which child it was, but we had lost one of them outside, towards the front of the building. Of course we were searching, and to our surprise the mayor himself brought this missing child back to us."

Times changed, but the essence of parenting is still discipline, love, guidance and communication. Grandma and grandpa did their best and they did an excellent job.

Chapter 5
Proverbs 11:30(The fruit of the righteous is a tree of life; and he that winneth souls is wise)

"Starting with myself, I began recording spiritual journeys about 1970. I was 48 years old. It was a spirit of growing, yet in reality, an immature desire or longing for a closer, intimate walk with my Jesus. It revealed itself in my prayer for each one of my children. Note: I began praying for any children God would give me."

"In February, 1974, we were living on Belmont Parkway NW in Cedar Rapids, Iowa. The children and I had gone to church and Gerald was home alone. It was then that God moved in on him and called him back, in no uncertain terms. God walked him back into the Free Methodist Church on G Ave., where he knelt down at that altar, repented, and surrendered to Christ.

"God took my husband back, and gave him a calling, 'Preach my Word!' Then in February, 1975, he was given by superintendent Wilson, a pastoral apprentice license. And in 1976, we began to minister at the Free Methodist church in

Newton, Iowa. Gerald preached and I taught. We had a very fruitful revival in the fall.

"In 1977, when we were 55 years old, we sold our home on Belmont Parkway, to answer a call to the Oil City Conference of the Free Methodist Church in Marienville, PA. At that time we were taking a Christian Education correspondence course from Winona Lake, Indiana. "Our family all grown we had a calling in Pennsylvania. We established our daughters, who had jobs, and they settled in an apartment in Cedar Rapids. Our youngest son Ben now in college in South Dakota.

"My spiritual journey was growing, but before I left Cedar Rapids, a bit of despair and at wits end, an excerpt from my journal. October 1, 1977. I just throw myself at the Lord's feet. Not knowing what to ask for. Just "Hoping in his Mercy." For two hours or more, just waiting. Praise his name, he came to my need. The next day, not knowing whence or how, the peace was there. My mind and heart at rest." (Psalms 142:1) I cried unto the Lord with my voice; with my voice unto the Lord did I make my supplication.

"All of this concerned our call to leave Cedar Rapids. I thought of my mother who is still here, and of course my children. How can I leave now? I am so proud or blessed of them all. I know they have faults and some difficult problems, but God is able about our children."

Her prayer for them:

"This day, November 10, 1977. "Bill, 30, so peaceful, strong, gentle and unmoved in God's word. Trusting all to God's promises for his ministry.

"Daniel, 29, so tender, gentle & compassionate, yet firm, staunch and full of zeal for the Lord, Jesus Christ. "Stephen, 28, God bless him. What a pillar of strength to me and comfort in his quiet assurance. "Trust Jesus", he said to me, and truth came shining through. There is much ahead for him, thank you Lord!

"Rose Mary, 23, so sweet, yet strong. So full of life, and wanting to use it. Music, singing, caring for the sick, bless her dear Jesus.

"Rebecca, 21, so alive, so eager to learn (college), so tender, yet wanting to cover it. Bless and strengthen her O Lord, let not the enemy or any foe keep her from your plan for her life.

"Benjamin, 19, son of our right hand, always strong, efficient, and ready to encourage. A quiet assurance. Strong in character. Bless him dear God, tonight, protect him till we see him again.

"And so it is this day, in a Ryder truck, with our green station wagon hooked to the back, we leave for Pennsylvania along with Bridgett our sweet dog. This is my prayer, Keep us Oh God, in the center of thy will. Bless our children, keep them and our grandchildren as well, we love and will miss them so!!"

In their absence, day by day, you can hear a yearning in grandma for her family. November 16, 1977. "Sad and lonely. I went to the mailbox , no mail! I've written pages and pages. Why? Thought sure some word from the kids or mother. Please God, let the girls write. Wonder if they are alright. Then relief. A letter and some pictures from Mart. A few days later Ben called, I miss him so. Ben won his last game at South Dakota University, bless and keep him Lord."

November 20th, 1977, again prayers going up for each of her children, and their individual needs. She takes the time to focus on her precious blessings.

"William George, bless Lord his ministry, and keep your hand on him and his family, always.

"Daniel Benton, Thank you for this son, bless and keep him always close to you Lord, as well as his family. Jesus give him a room for his use of his gifts for you.

"Stephen Joel, cause him to walk in thy way. Thank you for his gentleness and kindness. Bless him and his family."

"Rose Mary, so dear and sweet God, I miss her so, and feel I'm failing them being so far away. Please lead Rose, bring her out here to sing and praise you. She is yours Lord, remind her. She wrote, thank you."

"Rebecca Ann, so thankful for our precious Becky. Please call her again and again Lord. Her name means "called", and she needs you and your steadying hand. Bless and protect her from this rheumatoid arthritis."

"I just want to run home and make sure they are alright, it tears at my heart. I received sweet letters from Joel and Jenny, but why doesn't Daniel write? Sheryl will soon have the baby."

Grandma makes known to the Father above, every need for her children as well as her own peace in this time of separation.

Grandma & grandpa's pastoral duties to the church, in Pennsylvania, keep them active as she relates: "We came to Marionville on November 9, 1977, and settled into the parsonage. His word, the song in the house of our pilgrimage. A beautiful song of service there to children and adults. We had a lovely revival in May of 1978. During our sojourn in Pennsylvania we served in the Tidioute Free Methodist , East Hickory, and Newmansville, congregations. We served Bible study to a facility called, Abraxes. This was a site for delinquent youths and was a wonderful preparation for when we came back to Cedar Rapids, Iowa. So it was, in 1982 we returned to Cedar Rapids. Ministering and helping those in need.

"In 1984, we served and ministered at Quaker dale Group House, north of New Providence, Iowa. We served together, my husband and I, as house parents in a cottage for 10 boys, taking them to church each Sunday, working four days & having four days off.

"Then in 1987, we decided to leave Quaker dale. God had another place in mind. Gerald, at Larry Rutter's suggestion, took a job at Four Oaks, a children's facility in Cedar Rapids,

Iowa. Larry had worked at Quakerdale and moved on to work for Four Oaks and was a mutual friend. Gerald worked at Four Oaks as the day manager of the children, and the adult units until May, 1995. God blessing him in a spiritual program and Sunday school, as well as counseling for the children. While he was employed at Four Oaks we continued to minister a year; preaching and teaching at the Free Methodist church as well until 1992."

The Free Methodist church in Cedar Rapids closed in 1992. I remember feeling a sense of real loss. As their granddaughter it dawned on me that five generations had set foot in that small, brick chapel.

It all started with my great grandmother Daisy, bless her. Again, grandma and grandpa, started attending there in 1947. They brought their children up in this church and when living in Cedar Rapids remained members until the doors closed. That is forty-five years.

My dad, Daniel, married my mother there in 1968 and brought their three children into the congregation to be taught the word of God.

In 1990, my first son, Daniel Phillip, was baptized in this Free Methodist church. My first Sunday school teacher, Bessie Wilcox, remained there years after I had grown up. I felt a real security in that church. I thought it would remain always.

There was a true family and congregational heritage within those walls. It wasn't the richest church nor the most beautiful, but it was Bible preaching and Spirit filled. My daddy always told me that's what you look for in a good church.

The greatest teacher of all was my grandmother. She used the Word of God to equip us spiritually.

When I asked my grandfather how he and grandma felt when the church closed, he said: "Well, we were stunned, as they had asked me to preach for a year. We just thought things would continue to move forward, and of course our whole family had gone there. There was a bit of sadness with that."

With that, grandma continues with their journey: "Through our pleasant and blessed association with Shevon Webb, and the Redemption Baptist church choir, we met Pastor Harmon Webb and his blessed wife Anita. We transferred our membership letter to Redemption in 1992."

"Gerald took the necessary tests and appeared before Pastor Webb and Reverend Anders. Isaac Pledge was there as well. Gerald and Isaac were ordained on November 14, 1993, signed by Pastor Webb and Reverend Lewis Williams. Thank God for Jesus!"

Then grandma speaks of their time at Redemption: " Our coming up five year anniversary at Redemption Missionary Baptist Church will resound with joy. We have seen blessings and growth in our beautiful brothers and sisters in Christ. We have heard the joyful sound again and again. Thy statutes, have O' Lord, been my [our] songs in the house of our pilgrimage."(Psalm 119:54)

Grandma and grandpa ministered together as often as needed. Grandma once told me that they were truly at their best when they were ministering together, whether it be within the community or within the family.

I believe with any married couple, and in the best of marriages, there are things to overcome and situations to work through. The victory is, if you are truly of one mind, walking with the Lord, you will make it through the toughest of times. There are times when it seems one is carrying the other in Christ, and it is so important to hang on to the Word of God.

Grandma and grandpa were always, at least for me, a great example of a marriage in motion, working to accomplish one goal, just not always with the same angle. A letter grandma gave to me once, truly shows that struggle and demonstrates her faithfulness in seeking out the Lord in these times.

Grandma says: "Thank you for the scripture dear God. I know how much you've done for me and how near you are. I want to let others know. Help me!"

"Lord, what is it? Gerald is my husband. Every since we have been married, you've been with me. When he left for the army, the things I wrote admonishing him to stay close to you. I didn't always manifest perfection in my humanness, but you were there in my heart. Then when all the children came we cared for them, provided for them with labor, love and care. I guess I don't always fill his needs, but please let me know his caring for me."

"Jesus, you said man and wife were one flesh, and he that loveth his wife loveth himself, nourishing and cherishing. Dear Lord, we need a home, please, just a roof over us. Is it alright to pray this way? Holy spirit, instruct me according to Gods will."

These letters and experiences have helped me in my own marriage. I spoke to grandma many times of the frustration I felt in my own marriage. She would soothe and console me with her experiences and knowledge. After all, aren't we suppose to look to these elders of time, for counseling? We need more of this Christian testimony in this world today, to show us they too have struggled. I can't tell you how many times I sat with grandma and grandpa looking for spiritual guidance. I knew it would be based on truth and years of experience.

I can tell you, it truly "grows" you when your elders give you words of scripture to pick you up and help you to go on in time of need. I recall in 2003, grandma felt frustrated and called me for a shoulder to lean on. After we finished talking, I hung up the phone and was moved by the Holy Spirit to write a poem. I sent it to her to show her I felt her need and to console her spirit. It was a moment of growth in my marriage as well. Here is what God gave me to write:

"One"

Let foolish pride be still,
And our minds will reveal,
Beliefs-deep within our hearts.

Do you hear my tender words?
We have been apart.
Meanings,
Although they seem absurd,
I want to share,
Unconditionally.
I care.
Listen! Listen!
Please,
I really, truly, have a need.
Let knowledge be revealed,
As we remain together still.
Our views may not be the same,
But let us place no blame.
Let go those thoughts and be done,
Thus are minds reunite as one.

With each prayer grandma and grandpa came together. When I asked grandpa about their years together, he replied: "It was oneness in Christ, stepping out, ministering together, deciding together, then our problems were solved. We dwelled in the church and focused our ministry on young couples and families."

I wrote this poem for them, as a reward for their discipline in their marriage when Redemption Baptist Church celebrated one of many, of grandma and grandpa's anniversaries in Cedar Rapids;

"Golden Bond"

Golden is what they are,
And oh, how they have come so far.
Like a vine intertwined,
Nothing has broken them over time.
Working together as a team,
To achieve their many dreams.

Offspring great and strong,
Teaching us where our hearts belong.
Never easy, Never fair,
Even when the cupboard was bare.
Pulling and carrying through,
We can all see,
What we can and should do.
With Jesus along their trail,
Their true bond has never failed.

Now listen to that poem! That is what I have learned from them. What an example they have set for their family and others!

Now listen to this entry written by grandma to her faithful husband, October 5th, 1998, a personal insight on their 55 years together. Remember, with every thought from grandma, prayer and thanksgiving, come first, always.

"I got a new Bible today. Exactly like my burgundy one. It has been given to me by my heavenly Father. According as his divine power hath given unto us all things that pertain unto life and godliness, through the knowledge of him that called us unto glory and virtue. Oh, I love you Jesus, you have been so good to me, saving me, watching over me when I strayed, drawing me back and taking me through many things. Pain, sorrow, joy, hope and now Jesus, I am 76 years. How many, or what is the measurement of my days. Help me be strong and not afraid." So teach us to number our days, that we may apply our hearts unto wisdom.(Psalm90:12)

"Today being Gerald's birthday, I gave him his card, it is a very beautiful, timely one. You know after these fifty-five years together the most important thing I have learned is, that love is a whole lot more than flowers and candlelight! It's sticking together during those times when you are short on money, patience, and confidence. The sacrificing something you want for something the family needs and always being willing to listen. We have been through so much together and yet we have always emerged closer and stronger than before. I don't know if I could have made it through without you there by my side, you're my lover and friend. No matter what life holds in store. I can handle it as long as I have you. After 55 years we have given each other joy, we have given each other pain. But always in Jesus we've found our way again." Those that are planted in the house of the Lord shall flourish in the courts of our God. They shall still bring forth fruit in old age; they shall be fat and flourishing; To show that the Lord is upright: he is my rock, and there is no unrighteousness in him.(Psalm 90:13-15)

Yes, all those years grandma and grandpa shared it all, together. Even as they became older two separate people found a way to work together as one in Christ. They were still able to share intimacy as grandma shares with me at 81 years old. "Joel don't laugh. Love you"

January 9th, 2004:

"Woke up, Gerald with his arm around me. Here we are, two rested oldies at 81 years old, but still desire, and thoughts of marital pleasure engulf us. So in marriage, our bed undefiled, there is love. Then a beautiful thing!! Pleasure, like Sarah, who said, Shall I have pleasure? And then I said, "I felt that right to my finger tips. Then "we" like Sarah burst out laughing and I don't mean a chuckle, but a real deep down laugh. Abraham and Sarah brought forth Isaac, which means laughter. So I shall laugh as the years go on and thank our God, who loves us so. To provide for all our needs spiritual and physical, Amen."

Clinging to one another through the years, overcoming obstacles and coming together with each decision, for one unified answer, always in Christ.

Chapter 6
(Psalm 45:1 My heart is indicting a good matter: I speak of the things which I have made touching the king: my tongue is the pen of a ready writer.)

My grandmother was a very observant woman. This portion is for her. She was a wife, mother, grandmother and friend to others. Her care for others was deep and sincere. She knew that we are human and that "all have sinned and come short of the glory of God." She also knew that there is great peace when you ask Jesus for forgiveness. She faced her ordeals with her eyes on Jesus, and filled her heart with the Word of God to keep her from sin.

She was human, but she studied her Bible to show herself approved unto God, and thus she became worthy to teach others how to grow in Christ.

I took the time to look through all the writings, letters, and Bibles that my grandma had sent me. All of it overwhelmed my spirit. Such wisdom! So, Let me voice and share with you some of her thoughts, the inner woman. She was a strong woman, but she needed time for herself. As a child I didn't always see that. I saw the wonderful dinners, the awesome apple pies, the (Christ) centered Christmas celebrations. To this day, I can recall the old, worn nativity scene that she put up every Christmas. At the time they didn't seem old to me. They were comforting, and I subconsciously expected it every year. Then there was the soft Christmas carols she played on her worn record player. In the evening she kept the lights down low and there was a quiet time to reflect on the meaning of Christmas. Each year the Christmas program at the Free Methodist church was exciting to me to take part in the program. Though young, I began to recognize the spiritual significance, of this Holy observance. It always made me feel so proud to have grandma watching me perform on the stage. Gently smiling and nodding in approval. Each year I was an angel. Grandma always had praise and made me feel extremely special in my part. Then afterwards we would reflect on the events surrounding the birth of Christ.

As I grew older, I began to see Grandma the person; a person who also had needs, not just "Grandma". An intelligent women with goals and dreams who put great effort in everything she did.

Accomplishment in Christ was grandma's heart and soul. The world has lost a great one, but heaven has welcomed her home! She is now in the presence of Christ Jesus.

Darlene (Darling).Delight thyself also in the Lord; And he shall give you the desires of your heart. (Psalm 37:4)

Grandma stood firm in her beliefs. When it came to right and wrong, she could stand up with authority and put you in your place without one licken. I never perceived this as a bad thing; nor do I remember ever being mad at my grandmother. Her purpose was to serve the Lord, so her chastisement was admonition and nurture, with words of wisdom and integrity. Amen!

She drew strength from the Word of God. (Psalm 25:21) Let integrity and uprightness preserve me; for I wait on thee. She wrote Darlene next to this verse in her Bible. I can't stress enough how the Lord preserved her. He gave her strength and an amazing confidence to teach and speak His word right up to her last hours of life. I believe the words she spoke stayed with those she taught. Some can be more stubborn than others, but I believe her words about Christ have been received by all who were in her presence.

There are those who are out to change the world, but then there are the few, like grandma, who were out to save others, one soul at a time.

Her and grandpa use to say: "Just give them the word" (the Bible). Together they strove to hold forth the word, and save who they could along the way. There are many who don't know the Word, its plan for our life, the understanding it gives us, and the joy it brings to ones soul if we obey. Grandma always set out to make that very clear.

"Respect yourself!" A strong message, but perhaps there truly isn't enough of this in the world today. As women and mothers, we should get back to the Bible. Grandma voices her call to all women to respect themselves. This piece is a unique perspective from grandma, as she was unique herself:

Essence of a Woman

"Because of lack of instruction, a great number of young women today do not regard their bodies as a blessing.

"God took a rib from Adam and made a woman. The Hebrew for made, in this instance, is built. To make Adam he used the dust. In the Hebrew, Adam, by itself, always refers to mankind. The essence of woman was in Adam. God took it out and used Adam's rib on which to build a woman. Woman, a helper to Adam. The Lord formed man from the dust of the ground. Dust according to the Webster's dictionary is, a cloud of pulverized earth. You have seen clouds of dust in a storm, then see how it settles after a misty rain. God gathered up this dust, tempered it with a mist rising from the earth, breathed into his nostrils the breath of life, and man became a living soul. (Genesis 2:6-7)

"God looked and saw that it was not good for man to be alone. He needed one whom he could see. So God built a helpmeet, one he would call out of Adam, using his bone (a rib), and built the woman for him. A vessel suited just for him. God, who wanted everything good, gave special thought and effort into bringing out this wonderful personality and shaping it around the bone of Adam's rib. Clothing her with the flesh thereof. He caused a deep sleep, an anesthetic, if you please, for Adam, then removed a rib, and built the woman. God personally brought her to the man. Our Jerusalem Bible says, The man exclaimed, "This is to be called 'Woman,' for this was taken from 'Man.'

"So, women receive your blessing. You are special in God's sight. God said so. Women, let us stop trying to seek our own glory, which is not true glory. We are a special gift to the man, in God's eyes. Let Him help us reflect his glory, according to His Word. Holding on to your gift until the right moment with the chosen man. Becoming one in Christ, working together in Christ, and throwing out selfishness."

"Mothers, instruct your daughters to guard their bodies. In this day of seeking love through 'Easy Sex,' share with your daughter God's special blessing to them. He gave them a beautiful treasure. The womb, the place where life is engendered or brought to life. When the womb receives 'seed,' it is brought into life. Not waiting for life to begin. This womb is given only to the female. God's special gift is imparted with distinctive wisdom to grow and develop in the little girl, until the day comes for its ultimate, life cherishing task."

"Guard your precious treasure. Ask God for guidance in choosing your life companion. Believe me, he has a plan for that too. A right man for a right woman. As with all things, we need to ask, and wait for the right direction. For every male and female there is by divine design a right counterpart."

You are heirs, together of the grace of life. (1Peter 3:7) Likewise ye husbands, dwell with them, according to knowledge, giving honor unto the wife, as unto the weaker vessel, and as being heirs together of the grace of life; that your prayers be not hindered.

Man can pray and carry on, but if his love and attitude toward his wife are not right in God's sight, his prayers will be blocked.

"There was a time when doctor's, because of fear of malignancy, were performing hysterectomies, by their own admission, thinking of it as a preventive measure. Finally, some doctors began to realize the emotional scar it was leaving on a woman's heart and mind, as well as the body. In psychiatry, hysteria means violent, emotional paroxysms. This, ironically, is a description of the action of the womb when contraction begins for birth."

In Greek (hysterikos), hystera is translated, womb (uterus). The medical definition meaning: A disturbance of the uterus. Doctors began to realize that women were being deprived of their blessing, sometimes causing drastic after effects, physically, mentally and spiritually. Doctors became more cautious in advising a woman to have a hysterectomy. It can send the balance of a woman into chaos."

"As a precaution mothers, young women, again we say, guard your health, your precious treasure, your blessing from the Lord our God. Refrain from any drugs, alcohol, premarital sex, unnatural abortion. Anything that will jeopardize your wonderful heritage from the Lord. Look to Jesus Christ. He can and will help you plan and pray for the right one to be presented to you. Then in precious commitment, you both, as one, may bring glory to God."

Grandma was a spirit of grace, compassion, hope, and truth. A wonderful searcher of knowledge. Her writing's were full of detail. She studied well; She investigated words and subjects completely and to the utmost, from beginning to end. Each subject that God has presented to us has had her full attention at some point in her life. Whether it was science, mathematics, economics, literature or the Word of God. She truly enjoyed each research or project. She took her time in understanding all the wonders of the world. At times, there were tears of awe as she beheld God's Word in all of creation, and its unity. When she would tell me about these things, her inflection captivated my thoughts and pulled me in. Always speaking in a soft, slow voice with honest eye contact. You could see the passion in her sincere, expressive face.

God's grace was in her presentation of every subject, no matter how big or small. Nature and science were special favorites of hers. Grandma taught me very early on to appreciate nature and all its beauty. She said that it's a gift not to be taken for granted. It was evident in her Bibles. She pressed butterflies, flowers, simple feathers in her Bible, and used them for bookmarks. I could always find something lying between the thin pages of her Bible. Even pictures of loved ones.

Her book marks also reflected her personality and dedication to her Bible and books. Grandma loved her bookmarks. Always one present. Something so small yet ever so precious to her. She loved to receive a special book mark.

I listened to her and observed her ways. I didn't quite grasp it all until junior high, when science became fascinating to me. At times I was in awe of it all. I often said to myself, "Why didn't anyone tell me about these wonders of science?" When I would talk of what I had learned, she'd say, "Yes , isn't it wonderful how God made all things in his own way!" She made it very clear to me that all things, big or small, all, abound in the Bible.

Grandma took her Bible with her everywhere! Never hesitated, and no shame. She had a sense of confidence in the great scriptures. The Word was her supplication. As she relates in a portion from,

"The House of my Pilgrimage", in which she wrote:

"If someone should ask or should tell me, I must give up every thing except one thing, my heart would cry out, Take it all, but give me God's Word. It will never fail. Like Ezekiel, I have found it is in my mouth as honey for sweetness. As the sweet psalmist David said, 'Thy word is a lamp unto my feet, and a light unto my path.' I have surely found this to be so. The Lord has preserved my going out and my coming in these many years. I have nothing to boast of, only praise to offer Him for His mercy to me. My salvation through the precious blood of Jesus Christ of Nazareth, and the washing of the Word, making me clean. God's Word is the only precious portion we can give away and still keep. Praise the Lord! It is for everyone who hears the Call and will receive."

Mother Teresa said, "Holiness is not a luxury, you are all invited to it."

"As I said before, I do not know when this earthly house of this tabernacle will be dissolved, maybe soon or late. I do know I have a building of God, a house made without hands, eternal in the Heavens."

Grandma continues, "Today as I was thinking of Jesus' love and care for us, I thought how wonderful it is that if we were absent in the body, we can be confident we would be present with the Lord. So we labor that whether present or absent, we may be accepted of him." (2 Corinthians 5:9)

Ah, her love for books. She says, "I pause and thank the Lord for giving me a thirst for reading, and a deep joy in books. As I look back , even before school I was fascinated and thrilled by words, and the cover of books, and their titles. I can't think of his name, but I believe it was Lawrence Powell who said, 'Their covers seem to ooze with the juice of their contents.' They overflow with endless knowledge."

Her constant thirst for knowledge kept her very busy, and the Bible was always present along with her books. She had a deep research almost always laid before her on her dining room table. Usually more then one subject. She connected each subject to the next and always found something in the Bible to prove her findings in the content she was reading.

Now keep in mind she studied everything from the time she could read, so we're talking about a period of seventy-nine years, give or take. She would become so overwhelmed with joy when something would come together in her search for understanding. If you were there when it happened she'd say, "Come let me share something with you, but first lets pray. Then with those books stacked higher than her on the table, and the Bible in the other hand, she'd begin in a deep, soft, tranquil voice. Almost a near whisper. At times tears of joy in her enlightenment. Never forcing any words, but defining and simplifying in a slow masterful way. You never doubted she had done her homework!

As I said, grandma had a need to immerse herself in God's will. As she writes: "This is my desire to go deeper, to know what you want me to do, Oh Lord. Then give me the will and the strength to do it!"

She expressed this need in a poem:

"Not of Works lest any man should boast"

Go deeper, let Christ come behind the door, And change thy nature, and have thy innermost heart. Then with all His consummate art, He will remake you!! And lo, these lesser things, Shall flow as gracious rivers from pure springs."

"As I opened my Bible after typing these words, my eyes were directed to these precious words. In everything give thanks: for this is the will of God in Christ Jesus concerning you. (I Thessalonians 5:18) Thank you Jesus for all that has happened to draw me closer to you and all that is going to happen in your purpose for me." (September day of 1979)

Grandma always remained close to the Lord. Her spirit always reflected that. "Nobody knows the trouble I've seen." We've all been there; so low you can hardly pick yourself up. That's when we pour out our hearts to God, in secret; that's where we give him the hurts that only he can comfort, that's where we find it possible to forgive others and fulfill our needs in life. Grandma's writing, and her faith in the Lord kept her grounded and in control. Even her own human spirit couldn't always withstand this world. So she chose to seek out her Savior for abundant renewal and to help her grow. It is very clear in this poem:

"He Tempers the Wind To The Shorn Lamb"

I waited for the blow,
That was meant to give me pain.
It came!!! And lo! It only made me grow.
An angel, came between,
That blow and my trembling soul;
In surrender sweet, and sorrow keen,
I emerged! A heart made whole.
So welcome the blow,
That comes from the Master's hand,
In bruising and breaking, you understand,
Comes the strength to grow , again and again.
Till you come to full stature.
Perfect in the spirit of Christ,
Unique and whole, no fracture.
"One" in the Father and Son.

Darlene Long (November 17, 2000)

This poem comes from grandma's compiled work. She put it together in creative writing class at Cochise College in Benson, Arizona where she resided. She was very proud of it.

It was a her life long dream to go to college. She laid it aside to be a faithful wife and loving mother. Her excitement touched my heart, and I felt her passion to do this There was no hesitation or contemplating of her new adventure. But even more exciting to me was the fact that she went back to school at the age of 78.

Not to many seniors at this age have the energy and courage that my precious grandma had. She went into Cochise College on the wings of

her Savior. She was uplifted and had no reserves on what she was about to do. Not long before she started, she sent me a card. I could sense the stimulation in her being, a new beginning in her writing. She writes,

(Joel,

My dear, can't say I'm relaxed, as in laid back. I'm gung ho to go! It's official, tuition taken care of, praise the Lord. I get my used books August 7th or 8th. We have fixed the smallest guest room for my very own private study. I am so blessed! I love Jesus. He takes such good care of me! Your ever lovin' school girl!

Grand mere Darlene.

P.S. One of my classes will be 'Historic Indian Tribes of North America.

I was so excited for her. This was for her. Nothing to get in the way of her joy of books and learning. She absolutely loved it! When we spoke on the phone before she started, I could hear the motivation in her voice to fulfill something she always longed to do. The Lord and knowledge gave her great joy, and she wanted to share with all who would listen.

I read this from George Eliot: "It's never too late to be what you might have been." I think this fulfilled her desire for college that didn't happen when she was young. Although just a few courses I think it made her feel more alive.

Later in October, on the 1st, waiting for her test results, she writes to me: "My test went well. I haven't received the results yet, but I believe the best. No provision made for failure. Praise the Lord! I am full and overflowing in my writing class. Joel, I know I am a writer and shall go on 'til spirit, mind, heart, arm, fingers and pen are still. Then I can look forward to a writer's inkhorn by my side. Read Ezekiel , the 9th chapter. Could I also in linen have a writer's inkhorn?(A small container made of a horn to hold ink) an emblem of glory! Oh I love words and their origin."One of my best memories is the experience I shared with grandma and my family. We all went to the church camp grounds in Birmingham, Iowa. There was a natural peace there. A wooden tabernacle with the greenest trees of summer in the daylight, surrounded the grounds. The tabernacle was open to the outside on each side, letting the evening sounds of crickets and locusts in. You could smell and feel the moisture of the summer evening all around. The children could begin to learn and grow spiritually. The adults came together in great numbers for revival and fellowship.Members of the Free Methodist denomination from around the state were allowed to have cabins on the camp grounds and came together in the summer for a revival. There was also a kids camp. I attended it when I was a teen, truly enjoyed it each time.

Grandma and grandpa's cabin was basic and simple. One room with a hard wood floor. We ate off a worn, wood table; and I recall a porcelain sink, and an old squeaky bed that you sunk into when you sat on it. If I remember right, grandma had a couple of quilts on it that aunt Sylvie made.

This was a very peaceful place to me. It calmed my spirit. The preaching and singing in the open tabernacle. I remember the heat mixed with humidity of the Iowa summer, forcing one to be still; appreciating even the smallest of breezes brushing across ones moist face. The memory of the fun, stays with me to this day. This is just one of the ways she instructed me towards a relationship with the Lord, that is always etched in my heart. Building an awareness of his presence in good and bad times.

This day grandma is at the camp grounds in mid summer. She is in the Spirit. I can picture her sitting on the bed, or at the worn, wooden table in the cabin, dabbing her forehead, trying to keep cool. It 's July 17, 1990. She has a limited amount of light, and perhaps her eyes are closing ever so slowly. Her spirit deeply submitting in the obedience to the Holy Spirit. She has her Bible in one hand, and her pen in the other to record her inner most thoughts of the moment.

"Thank you dear Jesus, you have sent cooler breezes! While waiting quietly and thinking on your Word. John said you would baptize with the Holy Spirit and fire. I present myself, Lord Jesus, this part I must do. Present my mind, heart, soul and body. Dare I say it? A living sacrifice. Yes, I can in whole obedience to your instruction. Jesus, I beseech you, let me look upon you. I am tired of trying to 'refine' myself. Waiting O Lord, at the portals of this day. Let the operation begin, others! Yes, pray for others!"

"Gerald, O Lord, let reality, a realness embrace him. Let us be real in our relationship. Grow us together, Lord Jesus in 'perfect love' and unity. He belongs to you. I belong to you. You have brought us together. Let us walk in a perfect way, that we may serve you. 'The sit time has come.' Praise your precious name, Jesus. Look down from your sanctuary, on this camp ground , shake it O' Lord this day. Bless the evangelist, release him in truth, that thy Word will come forth with power.

"Remember my son Daniel this morning, dear Jesus, as he moves out with his papers. Baptize and release him, use the abundant Word you have given him. Supply his needs Lord. Oh God you provided for Israel in the wilderness, you can provide for Dan. I thank you Lord. Let his heart retain your Words in every way. An ornament of grace, provide this day dear Jesus, thy Word. Life to heart and flesh."

"Help me to bear witness of that light. Use me Father, or whatever is your pleasure. Perhaps I must observe someone else being used . A perfect natural flow of your Spirit in me. Keep me completely free in your truth. The real fasting of the preacher is not of food, but rather from eloquence."

In everything, grandma included prayer and praise to the Father above. She had an honest, daily sacrifice. Everyone who came into her presence was blessed under her anointed hands.

Grandma spent a lot of time in the library! She journals: January 19, 1998. " In the library today, I met this woman, divorced, husband lives in California, son is 14 and needs guidance. Must have been the Lord that brought us together. We discussed many things. She asked for my name and number and asked if she could call me?"

There were many of these little encounters in her life. Many souls were blessed because of her prayers and compassion.

As grandma grew older there came the time when she needed to have some of her teeth removed. I can recall her speaking of the anxiety she felt thinking about it. A few days before the procedure, her and grandpa stopped to see their son Bill. She sought the anointing from the Father above and receives it through her son and husband.

"Bill, bless him, anointed me with oil, he and Gerald, for my ordeal with the teeth pulling, and my heart and body were blessed."

We all had encouraged her to have it done. She prayed, and finally went, at the encouragement of her son Benjamin.

When the day came to have it done, October 22, 1998, she went to the Father and surrounded herself with these words, and notes it in her Bible as well. "I am getting prepared and trusting the Lord for his presence. It is here, the day at the dentist. He held my hand. This is my promise from the Lord." For I the Lord thy God will hold thy right hand, saying unto thee, Fear not; I will help thee. (Isaiah1:13)

Dr. Akey, a Christian, a gentle, empathetic, patient man. I have such confidence in his skill. I know God, Jesus, and the blessed Holy Spirit will be glorified!!! There were ministering angels when he began to put the numbing substance in with the needle, in four or five places, and then he began to pull the teeth. It was so blessed is all I can say! It left me relaxed and released. Out they came one by one, till he came to the front one that had the major problem, but praise the Lord it came out well. Finally they were all out and sutured. Then my new denture and partial neatly in place, with the gauze pads on each side to bite down on. Then we left, Gerald and I, we picked up my prescriptions for Motrin & Lotral for a pain reliever. I shouldn't have gotten them, I didn't need them,. Praise Jesus! I had some water, ginger ale and jello. I had to sit up in the chair. I had the "word" on my mouth. I woke up on Friday and took the antibiotic, the bleeding has stopped, rinsed my mouth and prepared to go back to see Dr. Akey at eleven o clock.

"When I spoke with him, he said I looked wonderful. We shared the scripture Isaiah 41:13-15. He smiled and was pleased! Went home took my medicine, ate some dressing, even chewed a little. Teach me Lord! Thank you! Later, off to bed and I took my new teeth out. One last word, It is impossible to please God without faith. Don't ever do anything without faith in Him.

"Woke up this Tuesday morning reluctant to put my teeth in. The Lord showed me. I had an ear to the devil's lies!! Yes, Lord Jesus forgive me. I told Satan to take his lies and his garbage and get out of my face! Praise Jesus! I am standing on His word. By his stripes, I am, my mouth is healed and he said, 'I am the Lord that healeth thee.' God's word is the key of life, anything but God's Word will kill you."

"Then on Tuesday , victory over the lies of Satan. I will not listen to his suggestions of fear and anxiety. I am right in Jesus' Word. He is holding me, healing my mouth to His glory."

"It's dark, thundering and raining. Showers of blessing. I made oatmeal, toast and a poached egg for Gerald and I. Lord,

Jesus help me to move my teeth. Help me with the partial and the metal, and how to chew, show me how to do it properly, thank you! It is in my heart to write a letter to Lisa. Help me Jesus with the words of certainty from your word."

Each grandchild was special to grandma. She prayed for each as their needs arose. "November 4, 1998, Lord help get my teeth adjusted, the sore spots, heal and quiet my mouth. Today is granddaughter Megan's birthday. Bless her Jesus that she will know you in a personal relationship." Grandma would say, "Everything has a purpose." (Ecclesiastes 3:1-8) To everything there is a season and a time to every purpose under the heaven. Every piece that she wrote reflected that as well. She would journal with a purpose and could sense when things weren't quite right. Born and raised in Iowa, she knew the cycles of the weather and loved every season.

November 30, 1998 she writes, "This is the last day of November and it is so warm, very out of season. Just as the Word of God says in Amos 9:13, Behold the days come, saith the Lord, that the plowman shall overtake the reaper, and the treader of grapes him that soweth seed; and the mountains shall drop sweet wine, and all the hills shall melt. It is like the seasons moving together, feels like spring, 70-72 degrees, and it's the end of November."

December 1, 1998: "It continues in the 70's, very pleasant, but not quite right. I long for the snow and so does my friend Vivian. Bless her. We have such wonderful fellowship together in Jesus. I talked to my daughter Becky, she likes the warm, but it isn't good for her animals. They think it's spring, the goats are shedding. All of nature is mixed up."

"Sunday has come and praise the Lord when we came out of church it was sleeting, with icy slush. Snowing and snowing, visibility not very good. We don't have church tonight. So we can stay in and rejoice in this quiet, warm home with beautiful white snow falling. Thank you Jesus! Vivian called. She was rejoicing in the snow fall as well. She told me she has been called to leave her church, Immanuel Baptist, just to stay home and receive whomever God sends. Bless her Lord Jesus. Keep her from harm. She is my dear friend, she is now 82."

"Early morning, December 18, prepared to go out to daughter Becky's. I made her favorite lemon delight. I spent some time with her, spoke of family and of Jesus' love and care. I love her so much. We read Hebrews 4, and Gerald prayed. I cleaned up our lunch and then we went home. I'm feeling tired and slightly on the sad side. When we arrived home there is what looks like a frame sitting by the door. When we got inside I opened the door, there so beautiful a picture framed in gold;

"The Invitation"

You are invited to come dine with me,
From now through eternity.
Believe in the Father, Son, and Holy Ghost,
And dine with Jesus as your host.
To live in heaven eternally,
All you must do is, R.S.V.P.

"Such an alabaster box (pitcher) of tears. The blessed Holy Spirit broke my spirit and the tears came. It was so healing, comforting and cleansing. The holy water ran down my cheeks in rivulets. Warm, loving and freely making little indentations on my face. Oh, such a blessing. Thank you Father and your blessed son Jesus, by your Eternal Spirit you share yourself with us, I love you. Thank you for Joel, this precious granddaughter. Order her steps in your word, O' Lord."

Sometimes emotion builds up in your spirit, feeling the burdens and disappointments of life. Then, someone comes along and does something that breaks the dam, and you cry. Then the Holy Spirit brings comfort. There have been times when I have done something or gave something, and really didn't know with what purpose. Times like these, I understand why. Grandmas give and give, but there are times when it just isn't there, and they too, need something or someone to fill their need. Sometimes, in order to give, we all need to receive. On that day I think that is what grandma needed, and there were many of these moments between her and I. Just simple, spontaneous sharing and giving. When she journals, I think it becomes her final release. I can almost feel it myself!

While going through all my keepsakes, I found a writing in which grandma returns to her home town, Coon Rapids, Iowa. It is a beautiful piece in which she reflects on the days of old. She makes you feel like you're walking back with her.

August 17, 1998

"Blessings, blessings, back to my home town. Such a lovely morning. Thank you Lord for strength in body and spirit to be able to do this. We are on the road again, just a few miles to Coon Rapids. Now I am 76 years old. I was 25 when Gerald and I left to settle in Cedar Rapids. With two boys, David and Bill. Now I have come from Panora where that one boy, Billy, is now the pastor of that United Methodist church. Thank you Jesus, how you have led us skillfully with your hand. Now we are coming around highway 141 past what use to be the swimming pool, now more modern with a golf course, beautiful. As I remember it, a little house near the swimming pool. Gerald and I lived there. My oldest was four years old and it was a very humble dwelling. I recall a tree close to the house. I remember a lightning storm one night. It hit with a flash and sent a round ball of fire through the house, striking the big tree and peeling the bark off. I recall thanking you Lord for your care! Gerald not following as close to the Lord at this time. I remember days when Gerald was at work, I would take my oldest David with a little red wagon that Nana gave Him (my mom) and in a little red suit she gave him. We would walk up the slight hill then ride down the hill together. It is a wonderful memory. Now I'm back some 51 years later with 7 children, 24 grandchildren, and

17 or 18 great grandchildren. That 4 year old now has a wife, 3 daughters and a son. That little boy Bill, well, he is now grown. He is now married to his wife Kendra, they have 5 children. Thank you my God for your mercy.

"Now, up that street past the old chicken house, across the track up to main street, Coon Rapids. A restaurant on the corner, the bank across the street. We turn left, there's the old "Garst" store, no longer, but the building is there. A flood of memories, picture flashes of the aisles of the store, the merchandise, the clerks, the dress department in the rear and the upstairs bathroom."

"On Saturday nights, my cousin Betty Jean Cory and I would go around the streets of our "hometown" carefree and happy. Thank you dear God for your hand of mercy upon me."

"Oh the popcorn wagon and Mr. Frolich's old store. Yes! Stern Mr. Frolich."

"Then across the alley, Armour's Creamery where my daddy George worked in the butter room. I can see him there in his white overalls and white shirt, smelling of butter and cream, taking care of the great vats of butter. I see his blue eyes and kindly face with brown hair, about 32 years old. He was diligent and faithful at his job! He would give us, Betty and I a nickel or dime to get popcorn or whatever we desired."

"Then Caswell's cleaning shop, all different now but same structures of buildings."

"Back down main street where the post office sits in the same place and the building where Mr. Cohen's department store was, as well as where everyone congregated to talk, townspeople as well as country folks. The Cohen's were Jewish, I didn't realize what I do now. Mr. Cohen was short of stature, typically Jewish and he could drive a close bargain, but always fair. Mrs. Cohen, a Jewish momma, Meriam, their daughter was in the class ahead of me. She was very talented and intelligent."

"Then there was Whitten's drug store. It was always a cool and exciting place. As you walked farther back into the store there was long, tall shelves that held mysterious and interesting pharmacy. Mr. Whitten was friendly, dignified and a little bald. It seemed like he was always ready to talk to youngsters like me. There was the soda fountain which brought forth sweet, colorful shakes and sodas, and oh that yummy ice cream." "There was a cash and carry grocery store, Ted Mozena the proprietor, had a wide smile and was very friendly."

"And of course the Lyric theatre with a little restaurant along the side. You stepped up to go to the theatre box office to buy your ticket, then into the lobby towards the dark interior. Seats on each side which were wooden seats with arms. As you were there longer your eyes became accustomed to the dark that really had light in it. At this time I was only about seven or eight and there were still some silent movies. The 'talkies,' they called them came in the late 20's and 30's. The picture was up on the screen, people speaking on the screen . Then beside it was a piano player, who was on a platform playing the timely music. It was an amazing thing to everyone at that time."

"Now to the south side of the street, buildings all here, but different businesses and people 50 years later."

"On the south side on the corner there was an oil station where Spider Wallace worked. He was the older brother of Clayton, my kindergarten playmate."

"Then there was the south side Café, a red building with a big black door. Inside the door, a case with gum and candy bars, where a four or five year old could stand and yearn while the adults paid their bill at a "cash register", not a computer! Then the great big mirror behind a white marble soda fountain and of course the counter where several business men and employees came for coffee and rolls."

"Then Bryan's variety store. It was such a delightful place, the woman who owned it was plump, jolly and patient. Especially when you only had so much to spend and there were so many things (trinkets), but so beautiful to children as well as adults. Up above that store was Dr. Collard, the town osteopath, she could rub away those pains. She had wonderful white hair, a kind face and big, black, horn rimmed glasses."

"Oh and the South Side Pool Hall. Betty and I always walked cautiously and ever so quickly past this establishment. It smelled of beer, with whiskered men and loud talking. On down the main street of Coon Rapids, my favorite place even then at the age of seven or eight and through high school. Know what? The library! My transport to places I would only dream about, old times. Five Little Peppers, Treasure Island, Pilgrims Progress, Thoreau, Walden, Tom Sawyer, Shakespeare, Wordsworth and so much more, I read them all. On rainy afternoons I could be found in the library. Mrs. Browning was the librarian, she was the typical, helpful assistant, with soft, brown hair pulled back into a bun. The smell of books intrigued me. I wanted more and more. I guess my life may have been lived a little to much in books. I was a little to timid or fearful after my daddy left us to step out and actually do what I read about."

"God was truly my Father. Again as he said, 'I'm a father of the fatherless.' When I confessed my sin at eight He heard, and from that day on He watched over me. So his word became my life and still is at seventy-six. Oh, I have learned so many lessons and I thank Him, even today I find blessing and refuge in books in our Cedar Rapids library, a large stone building with sliding doors that open automatically, as you step before them into a cool atmosphere, drawing you into that sweet smell of books. Even in the entryway, a quiet satisfied sigh comes from the depths of my soul, as you anticipate the wonder of them all."

"Then on up the street and around the corner, up to the shoe shop and the Tuel home where mother and I lived upstairs in 1937 after my father died."

"So we drive now in 1998 over and by all these places. Then to the city park, which is now Thomas Rest Haven. We visited Gerald's sister-in-law, Mozelle Long (Lois), and we prayed with her."

"Then we left and went down to 141- lunch place and had a huge tenderloin, cottage cheese with French fries, tasty. We had a nice glass of lemonade. Then we visited houses I had lived in. The house on 6th street particularly special. I was very happy here. My daddy came home at noon for lunch and mother always had a beautiful, clean house with lunch prepared. After we ate he would sing, and very well. Black face songs. "Now Honey You Stay in Your Own Backyard", and "A Preacher Went a Hunting." I was a about eight and it delighted me. I'd say, "Sing it again.""

"Here at this house mother and I attended the "Assembly of God" church. The spirit quickened me, I acknowledged my sinful lost condition and Jesus saved me. We did attend the Christian church, where my dad went forward and was later baptized. Thank you Jesus, he is in your care. Again mother and I lived on God's Word, literally read certain Psalms every day before we ventured out to face the world (our town) in the 30's. If you, whoever you are reading this, grandchild or other. Please let Jesus have your life completely. He is so faithful, kind and loving."

"As Gerald and I begin to leave Coon Rapids we stopped at "Willow Cemetery." Through the gate and down the path by the fence. It is summer now, but my mind, my inner eye, sees January. It is cold, gray and the snow is covering the ground, with ice crunching under our feet. It isn't real to my eleven year old heart. A shock to mother and I. I watched grimly, shivering in the cold, tears wouldn't come. Why? Why was my daddy gone? What were we going to do? Go on, of course. Mother and I were very close. There is the "Cory" stone. My great grandfather, grandfather, and my daddy George Cory. My father now has been gone 65 years. I look up and leave a prayer, "Mercy Lord Jesus! You know all hearts and I leave a cross and flower, it makes me feel better.""

Grandma had deep feelings for her father. She carried him in her heart her whole life. There was an ache in her voice when she would talk of him, and her loss at such a young age. There was also a great voice of pride when she would speak of his love for her. She left it in God's hands to what his fate would be and leaned on the Lord. Grandma wrote many pieces. The ones that excited me were the ones in which she went deeper into her imagination and studied the subject with heart. She had several opportunities for that in her creative writing class. Especially when words were examined. She taught me to study well. I find myself doing it often. I observed the way the way she studied things that were beyond her knowledge. Her desire to know.

"A Sense of Wonder I don't Quite Understand"

Wonder: "A person, thing or event that causes astonishment and admiration. A marvel, surprise, awe, miraculous." (Webster's Collegiate Dictionary)

"Just before I board that huge, live, almost breathing hulk of metal before me, they tell me it weighs approximately 875,000 lbs. I am seized with wonder. I am awed by this miracle, this natural movement of air, this force that defies gravity. This force acting on a body, equal to the mass of the body. The plane multiplied by the acceleration of gravity, the increase of velocity per second. Yet I do not understand or analyze that awesome moment when I sense, feel and experience the giddy delight of being airborne!!" "Another sense of wonder at what I do not quite understand. I don't understand the ebb and flow of the ocean waves. Obeying the decree made by our Creator, God, that the waters should not pass his commandment! Saying, hitherto shalt thou come, but no further, and here shall thy proud waves be stayed. Again that giddy ecstasy seized me as I stood ankle deep on the shore of the Pacific ocean. Seeing those mighty waves coming in and knowing they could go only so far and no further. I thought of Robert Frost's poem:

"Once by the Pacific"

The shattered water made a misty din,
Great waves looked over others coming in.

And thought of doing something to the shore,
That water never did to land before.
But could not because of the,
Creators decree.

Robert Frost

"Another wonder, I do not quite understand. My eyes look up, I behold the clouds, visible masses of condensed water vapor suspended in the atmosphere, consisting of minute droplets or ice crystals."

"I watch amazed at their shape, the continuity of their motion, the change of colors."

"Our creator asked Job if he knew the balancing of the clouds? They have a purpose for balancing our earth. The clouds pour down rain, according to the vapor. Can we understand the spreading of the clouds or the noises of the thunder. There is light in a cloud, which now overwhelms me with the glory of the rainbow. The wonder I do not understand is the working of his light in the cloud. But science agrees when the suns rays meet a raindrop, most of the light passes through the center of the drop, but the light passing through the upper and lower parts are refracted, bending and splitting into its seven component colors, producing a rainbow. I do not perceive completely, but I see red, orange yellow, green, indigo, and violet, and know."

"When sunlight dances with the rain it's wonderful. A gift wrapped for a moment in the sky. Too beautiful for words, we are called to silence, awe and praise for our Creator."

I love the way my grandmother thought, so unique. Perhaps it wouldn't fascinate me as much if we hadn't spent so much time together over the years. I can't help submerging myself in her words of truth and understanding. How age does come quickly, as she holds onto it, revealing it will come again!

Joel M. Mulholland

"Let Me Wonder"

Wonder holds my youth,
I shall not let it go.
It sparkles in a tear of truth,
And quickened, begins to grow.
My body responds to the clock of ages,
Each tick brings a change most evident.
Wonder revives and defies the sages,
Youth renewed, by heaven sent.

Darlene M. Long

The wheels in grandma's mind were always turning with wonder and discovery. She knew that we were just discovering things which were already there, especially in science. She would always say if scientists would just look to the Bible it would come full circle. She wrote to me in October, 2003:

(Dear Granddaughter,

I guess this is a prayer letter. These words certainly not originally my own. Like Solomon in Ecclesiastes 1:9-10.
(The thing that hath been it is that which shall be, and that which is done is that which shall be done: and there is no new thing under the sun.)
Please read this with Ecclesiastes 3:15. (That which hath been is now; and that which is to be hath already been; And God requireth that which is past.)
So! Please think on these things my dear one.
In regards to letters, today you have computers. In the past, there were letters. Oh, Joel your grand mere treasures her letters like the early morning sun. We as Jesus' followers are to be letters to the world, of his love. A sort of Valentine from God to a love hungry world. As Macrina Wiederkehr says, Let us keep alive and treat with respect the joy of letter writing. Take time to do this, remember this is actually prayer. It is also prayer to

68

receive and read a letter. Part of your spirit breathed into the envelope, our soul. "Love" invisible yet so real.

Well dear one, I needed to relay that to you. As love is what we are really sending when we send a letter to a loved one.

Grandmere,
Darlene)

Grandma had box upon box of letters. I know they were her treasures. She would say how much fun it was to go back and pull one out from years back and read it over again.

I recall sending her a letter typed on my new computer. When she received it, she called me and said, "Joel, it's nice that you got a new computer, but I prefer seeing your penmanship. I don't see your presence when it is typed."

I got what she was saying. No two peoples handwriting is the same. It is their own, so personal, so intimate. Like a hug from their soul, in an envelope. I think any true writer can relate to that. In a phone conversation with my son Colin, she commented on a hand written letter with a poem that he had sent to her;

"Colin, your Bio-poetry, wonderful! Such insight and honesty in expression. A writer must possess these qualities. I love its essence and will cherish it. I will be looking forward to more in your own hand and heart writing."

"See, computer printing can't carry that essence. It's the taking the time to write it out, and sending it on, to say, "I'm thinking of you, and I want you to know that carries that essence in the absence between me and thee."

Grandma loved the letters she received, and she loved to write them in return. She filled them with scriptural definition and instruction. No two letters or card she wrote were ever the same. She never sent a card with just a signature. The whole card on the inside was filled with her love and instruction. She spent a lot of time in the card isle in stores. No one she loved was ever left out in receiving a blessing in an envelope. Thank you Lord for her words and lessons that help each of us to carry on in this world. One day I hope to have fellowship in letters with her again! (2 Corinthians 10: 11, Let such an one think this, that, such as we are in word by letters when we are absent, such will we be also in deed when we are present.) Grandma's words or letters were powerful because they were of Christ, period!

Chapter 7
(Ruth 1:16 And Ruth said, Entreat me not to leave thee, or to return from following after thee: for whither thou goest, I will go; and where thou lodgest, I will lodge: thy people shall be my people, and thy God my God.)

At what age do you grow close to your grandmother? I was very young. I was about two or three according to my aunt Becky. Becky was very close to me. I spent a lot of time with Becky when I was growing up. I remember staying with grandma & grandpa quite often. Grandma was always near, especially when I grew close to her My heart would absorb her wisdom. I loved being with her, and when I wasn't, I wanted to be.

Later in life grandma enjoyed telling me about how, when I was two or three, I stood up on a stump at the park and hollered, "Praise the Lord!" She said it was then that she knew the Holy Spirit had taken hold of my soul. She began to nourish and teach me according to my intelligence. At each stage of my life giving me a little more to digest. Giving me the pieces to understand the world around me, and how the Word of God must be present in all things we see and do.

I can recall things from back to about four years old. Sometimes my senses throw me back to the smell of her kitchen in the morning. The roasted coffee in a perking coffee pot, toast, something cooking. Perhaps oatmeal or Malto Meal. Setting the table according to the meal. She had a precise and delicate touch. There was no rushing in her prayer or presentation of each meal. This was not tolerated, and she would say so. "Eat slowly, don't rush. Sit down here, what's the hurry? Let's pray and read a few verses before we start the day."

If she knew you were coming to spend the night with her she would make it comforting. The guest room prepared with crisp, clean sheets and placed on the bed just so. Often with a freshened quilt. The hospitality made you feel special. At the end of the evening, a final prayer. Reassuring us that we were surrounded by the love of Jesus. Then a quiet goodnight and a hug. Sleep would come with warmth and a sweet dose of serenity.

Grandma's Bible was always present, and the first reading of the morning was from the Word of God. I didn't always understand what she was reading, but she was instilling something in me, and it felt good and peaceful. If there are any words that she spoke that stand out the most it would be: "Jesus loves you Joel." always in a soft, gentle voice. I can't count how many times she said this to me through out my life. Four words resounding as a hymn in my spirit. It was and still is etched in my consciousness. Especially the expression on her face and in her devoted, sunken brows. The intense eye contact in her blue eyes that looked me directly in the eye. It was compassion and concern for the salvation of my soul.

I don't recall ever being awake and up before grandma. She was up when I went to bed and up when I awoke in the morning. She rose and began with her daily devotion. She loved the stillness of the morning. She was usually up before anyone and cherished every minute. One morning she wrote: "Reading in Deuteronomy now. I have read about 10 chapters this morning, at the edge of my bed. Just leisurely meeting the day, Oh God what does it hold?"She started every day with her faith in God. The same in the evenings. She always read and prayed at the end of the day. At times her days would end after midnight, falling asleep on the couch, or in a chair with her Bible laying open on her chest and her hands laying folded over the word. I found this little saying somewhere. It mirrored her day. "If you hem in both ends of your day with a prayer, it won't be so likely to unravel in the middle." I'm not sure who wrote it, but it certainly is a reflection of grandma.

I loved to go on walks with her, even when I grew up. When grandma and grandpa lived on Belmont hill, in Cedar Rapids, Iowa. I was between four and six years old. Sometimes, in the summer, we would walk down the long, hot, dusty road to where her sweet friend Vivian lived. Maybe we would stop and say hello, then walk down the path behind Vivian's house, over to Belmont park. We would walk up and down the hills usually with her precious dog Bridgett running ahead of us with the excitement of being free outdoors.

I recall some of the hottest days of the year, we'd still walk to the park, sweating in the heat of the summer, and we would have a picnic. She would lay a blanket down on the ground while she took our treats from the picnic basket. Then we would move on to the wading pool. She would pull the bottom of her pants up to her knees while dipping her feet in the cool relief and splashing the heat off her face. Meanwhile I was immersed completely in the pool. Finally feeling relief from the overwhelming moisture. Other times we would have family picnics. She would have everything prepared, and she always knew how much. She would put it in a picnic basket along with delicious side dishes and off we were to the park of choice. Those days were filled with joy having my cousins there to play in the freedom of being a child.

Usually these occasions included aunts, uncles, and cousins. My cousins from Cedar Rapids are close to my heart. We spent a lot of those times together playing, laughing, and sometimes we were just out right ornery. Grandma almost insisted on these family picnics, and it seemed to keep us close together. These picnics weren't always perfect, but many memories came from grandma's meals. Whether in a park or a backyard, for all these gatherings she made sure everything was in place, with table clothes placed on the wooden tables, just right. No hurrying of course. Then always a special prayer for the meal, and the time together as a family.

Despite some those sizzling summers, it didn't bother me when I was with her. Regardless of my age or what we were doing, even if it was nothing at all, all those moments were priceless. Grandma could always find a way to fill my empty moments.

The area where grandma lived on Belmont hill was out away from the inner city. It was out far enough to get a sense of the country. I loved it.

On each of our walks together, grandma and I would talk about the skies and the heavens, trees, birds, the weather, even sound of the birds to the aging of the trees.

Looking at a tree stump one time, she pointed out a little mystery to my young mind, "See these rings Joey? Each one represents the age of this old tree." I can't think of any marvel of nature that grandma didn't introduce to me. Including our own bodies.

I often recall those summer days and all the joys of being with her. She would climb on the jungle gym with me which excited me that she took the time. While proving to me she could climb up that playground equipment. We leisurely discussed little things. I was curious, and my little mind needed to know. She would say with a whisper, "Can you hear that? That is the morning dove, "coo coo." To this day, if I hear a dove when I am walking or napping with the window open, it instantly makes me think of my grandma, and it brings a calmness and peace over me.

Grandma instilled in me the importance of the little things in life. The things that really matter, that people take for granted.

She would talk in a slow, quiet voice as she explained something to me. She always took time, no matter what she was doing. She never hurried with an explanation of how God created things and set things in order. We would pick flowers, smell them and take some back home to press them in a book or her Bible. In Spring, of course we had to pick lilacs and place them in a vase, in the middle of the dinner table.

It was always exciting to go places with grandma. When I rewind my thoughts, I recall going shopping with her, eating at Killian's department store and even going to a symphony once. The place we went the most, was the library. She'd lean on my arm and we'd talk about our thoughts for that day. When I was little, I must have spent hours and hours with her in the old library. The smell of all the books mixed with the stuffy smell of the old building, and the old, iron, steam heaters. I observed the heavy, black iron rod doors and elevator. The atmosphere felt mysterious to me. I recall it as if it were yesterday.

Grandma taught me to love and appreciate reading. There was always a thirst and excitement for knowledge in her eyes as she would open a book. At times, running her hand across the top of the book in appreciation of her precious nugget she hadn't quite tasted and savored yet. She always took notes and had written summaries of what she had read. Then sharing what she had read with others.

I came across a quote by John Adams, stamped on an envelope not to long ago. I couldn't help thinking, this is grandma. "Let us dare to read, think, speak and write." Grandma continuously spun her web of knowledge in this cycle, her whole life. This eventually captured many of our hearts. The difference? The

Bible was her source, along with her books to complete her understanding of all things to pass on to others.

There was always a stack of books on her kitchen or dining room table, with a cup of coffee or cappuccino. Oh and we can't forget the pen she always held in her hand. Never far away. Grandma was a fountain of knowledge to me. Many times I would ask her things, but she would make a full project out if it, with no detail missed.I went to her often over the years when I needed guidance and an understanding of life. The fear of the Lord is the beginning of knowledge: but fools despise wisdom and instruction. (Proverbs 1:7) This is so true and grandma would tell me God and knowledge should always be kept together. That is why you always saw her Bible right along with her books. I find myself doing the same thing as I get older.

Grandma insisted church be a part of her children's lives, and many in the family grew up in the Free Methodist church. Together, Grandpa with grandma leaning with her arm inside his. Then grandpa removing his precious cowboy hat when entering the church with courtesy. Then up the inner stairs to the ushers to place their offering As time went on some stayed and others went their own way. When grandma & grandpa lived in Cedar Rapids, that is where they went until it closed; as well as my dad. At times grandma taught my Sunday school class. I recall some of my cousins coming once in awhile. My cousin Cindy and Iwere talking one day. We recalled some of the moments at church. We'd sit in the pew close to grandma and grandpa. At times we'd get antsy and we'd talk out of place. Our grandfather would throw us a look. We knew that we had better stop. If you sat close by grandma, all was well. If you got caught more then once for bad behavior you sat beside grandpa and you knew not to get out of line. If you messed up again, you were taken by the hand and marched outside on the church steps. You didn't want to go there. You had a swat waiting for you.

I'm almost sure that at some point, all of us grandchildren, and even the great grandchildren, have received a Bible from grandma with a special writing or note in the front of it. The first one she ever gave me was a big one, and it meant more to me then gold. I believe I was ten. I use to love to sit next to grandma and grandpa in church, and I would look through her Bible and find so many different little things in it. You could be sure that there were four or five dainty flowers pressed between the pages with little sayings or poems written inside the cover that she wished to remember. Then I would joy over getting a piece of gum from her. No doubt about it, had to be Wrigley's Spearmint or Juicy Fruit. If she wasn't at church for some reason or another, it was so disappointing to me, although it was very rare.

Of course, who, but grandma was there when I went to the altar to ask God to forgive me for my sins. I was not forced, but it was my appointed time. Grandma bent down at my side and we prayed. To go forward is a huge step in one's life and for her to be at my side was extremely special. As prayer was said, she whispered, "Yes Jesus, keep Joel in your hands," such protection.

In 1976 grandma and grandpa moved to Pennsylvania, I was only six years old. I will never forget the day they left. They packed up the Ryder truck, and I remember kissing them goodbye. My heart nearly broke and sank into a deep emptiness. I couldn't see or talk to her, and it really bothered me. I had never been without her for a long period of time. I felt a real void in my little heart and mind. I recall crying and not being able to control it. I must have written her a million letters while they were out there.

In 2001, grandma sent me a package, and inside were a whole stack of letters I had written to her. One was a piece of notebook paper with a bouquet of roses cut out of a magazine, with these words written on it: To grandma. I love you. You are the rose of my life. Love, Joel. Years later, grandma wrote on it,

"One day Joel this comforted me! Now, I return it in 2001, its message engraved deep in my heart, lovingly." Now, as I look through them and read them, I feel a yearning to see her. Such innocence. This one in 1977 so touched me.

(Dear grandmother,

I'm so sad that you are so lonely. I hope I get to see you. I was crying so badly. I love you.

Love, Joel)

I was only six years old. When I look upon some of these letters, I see such seriousness for my age, but with a realness that even now makes my heart hurt. As in this one from 1980:

(Dear Grandma,

I will soon be living with my dad. I hope I can still come to Pennsylvania to live with you for awhile this year. Grandma, something strange has happened to me. I keep thinking that my dad is smoking. This is Joel talking. Sorry I haven't been writing to you. I went to see great grandma Kirk and she was tickled pink. She was really looking good. Here is a list of things I want for Christmas. A watch, a set of books, a set of lip smackers and a radio.

My dream came true grandma. I get to live with daddy. I hope other dreams will come true. I want to live with you for awhile, because I love you a lot grandma.

I am going to be 11 in four more months. I've gotten seven book reports done. How is grandpa? How is it going at your church? I have been going to church at the Free Methodist. Please write to me and tell me how it's going over there. Please send me a picture of you and grandpa.

Grandma when I think about the things we did together, it hurts me because I didn't want you to move away. When are you guys coming back to Iowa to see everybody? Oh, how is

Bridget? She must be getting old by now. She has had a lot of puppies.

We are learning some new things in math and it is fun. We all went to Camp Wapsie Y, both the 5th and 6th grade classes. We all had fun. We got to make baskets and watched movies. Well I hope you enjoyed my letter. Oh, here is my new address where I will be when you write to me. I am writing this at school.

Love, your granddaughter,
Joel Long)

With each of my letters to her, there is a progressive maturity in my writing and a need to see her more and more. As well, my Christian upbringing was growing. I so needed to be like my grandma, and I felt I needed her at my side. That was just the pure innocence of the child. Isn't it funny, as we grow older we pull away from those we are closest to, even if it is just a little.

This next letter, my faith is growing. I was attending church, and CYC (Christian Youth Camp) each year, and as I said, it is a very special memory to me. Especially because my uncle Bill was there, and he was such a peaceful, quiet assurance to me at that time. I always felt such love for all my family, and I made that very clear to grandma in this special letter:

(Dear Grandma,

How are you? I love you and miss you guys very much. I want you guys and the whole family to know how much I love all of you. I do love you grandma, and I love you grandpa.

I'm going to CYC camp this year, in June. You guys, I hope you know I'm becoming a real believer in Christ. I go to church on Sunday, and I read my Bible every day. I'm glad I have mostly Christians in my family because I would hate to see any of them go to hell. I must go.

Love,
Joel)

All my letters to grandma were so open and honest. It was always that way. When my parents divorced, it really affected me. It felt dark and awkward. At that particular time, life didn't seem fun at all. I wrote her often about it. Emotionally, it was very hard on me to no longer have my daddy with me all the time. She always seemed to walk me right through it, and helped me tremendously in my teenage years.

She wrote sweet little words in her cards that always made me feel so special. "Joel, There was the day when you were three. So sweet, so winsome and carefree. Days have come and gone so fast. Our love is strong and will always last. You are sixteen now, still sweet and winsome. May the next sixteen years bring you joy and dreams come true. Let Jesus guide and always be happy in him."

Cards were always constant between us. It was nothing to send two or three a week. I truly loved picking them out, making a true effort to find something that she would love. It didn't matter if she was across town or thousands of miles away. We always corresponded on paper! A lot of true feelings poured out into our cards. We looked for those letters everyday in that mailbox.

I recall the feeling I had after I came home from laying grandma to rest. I told my daddy, "This sounds crazy, but every time I go by the card aisle I want to start crying. I feel like I have no reason to go down that aisle anymore. A gut wrenching emptiness comes over me when I go to the mailbox knowing I won't receive any cards from her."

I could spend a half an hour in that aisle, picking out the best card for her for that moment in time. We always seemed to sense what the other needed. Cards were a huge communication tool. Sometimes when you couldn't say it out loud, it was easier to write it out and everything would flow right from the heart. I looked forward to each subject and scripture she would have to tie in with her thoughts. Each having such substance that brought great understanding. Here she writes:

May 25, 2000

(Joel Marie,

A little face, sweet eyes of blue, have followed me the years so true. Our hearts entwined, our spirits kin. We share the deepest feelings within. Anticipating each sigh and fear, we mingled such sweet tears. Growing together, age and youth, the whole complete. My love abides here, Joel, in Jesus always. Be strong dear one, I know you will. By the way grand mere causes me to feel regal, like a queen that is. Remember this one in prayer.

Tenderly,
Grand mere Darlene)

I always loved to call her grand mere. I picked it up in high school in French class. It does have a bit of class to it.

Grandma loved to get cards from everyone. It was hard, in this particular area, for someone else to get cards and not her; keep in mind cards and letters were treats to her soul. I had sent one to grandpa one time and when he received it, she certainly took note. In her next letter to me she wrote: "Grandpa loved your card, and I can't resist this. No I won't say it. I didn't get any, ha! Until the next day. Remember, every morning there is a kiss on your cheek as a prayer ascends, shedding Jesus' light on your day!"

An awesome grandma, her heart never hardened . She always ended each letter with a comforting word that carried me for days, and a soft reminder that our hearts should always be looking to the Lord. For if we are right before him, we can love without a hardened heart. Not because it's mush, but because Jesus said so. We are suppose to love one another, but there were times she felt the sting of rejection.

Many prayers and tears filtered through her love as she prayed and waited on the Lord. I admired her for that. Instead of hating someone she prayed it through. She would say, "you mustn't hate anyone Joel!"

I went to one of grandma's Bible not long ago to find the verse in Matthew to quote pertaining to her thought on loving those that hate you. When I went to Matthew 5:44, I couldn't believe it. She had already noted this on the page with an "x" next to verse 43 and 44. (Mt. 5:44) But I say unto you, Love your enemies, bless them that curse you, do good to them that hate you, and pray for them which despitefully use you, and persecute you. But it shouldn't surprise me that she had it noted. Now I know why she was such a guidance in my life. She knew the Word, and what scriptures were to be used in every circumstance! I always felt security in her knowledge of the Bible.

Grandma wrote a lot of letters, but she received many over the years as well. She kept them all. There were boxes and boxes of them. She loved to look back through letters from the past. She seemed to use them later for her need and for others as well. She sent me a letter when I was fifteen expressing her thoughts on this, August 24, 1985:

(Dear granddaughter,

It's later, or I should say, "early" in the morning. I've been sitting here going through a box of cards I've kept down through the years. Birthday, Mother's day, anniversary and Valentine's day. Many from our children and also grandchildren. I read the little notes inside, and my heart is thankful for each one. How God has blessed us.

Joel, let Jesus have all of you and walk each day with him. What joy, what surprises, what delights he has for us, and we can serve him with joy forever.

Well dear one, I love you very much. Remember us in prayer the next week.

Love and blessings,
Grandma Long)

When grandma wrote to me I often felt the elderly responsibility in her words. I don't see that these days. It was a natural for her and she never worried about offending us. She always brought out the truth and put us in check when she felt we were doing something wrong. She was very adamant about walking right with the Lord.

"Joel, put Jesus first! In all facets of your life. Be obedient, whatever is required of you. to be first. Be God's woman, a good wife, mother, and a witness for Jesus Christ, wherever you are. "

Through all those teenage and marriage experiences, disasters or joys, grandma was always there to encourage and praise me.

August 20, 1996 she writes:

(Joel,

Granddaughter, In my heart you hold a special place, since you were just a tiny girl. Your spirit and mine, found a resting place in Jesus. I know you went through the restless years, but Jesus' presence has been with you, rescued you, blessed you and carried you. Gently let Jesus shine through your life. For your husband Kevin and your two wonderful sons, Dan and Colin. They will rise up and call you blessed, and your husband will praise you.

Once again, dear granddaughter, you are very special, and I love you. Remember me in your prayers.

Love,
Grandma)

As I got older, I started to recognize grandma as a person. Not just my grandma. I started to see the effort she put into everything and how tired she would be at the end of the day. We'd sit on the sofa and at times she would say, "Oh my feet." I could see the course of time and labor had taken its toll on her worn, swollen soles. I'd rub them for her, and you could see she enjoyed the pampering. Over time they became dry. Corns that had built up on her feet screamed, "Remove me!"

We started to enjoy the same things and appreciated the little things together. Again, I grew to really enjoy the sound of the "coo" that the dove makes, and every time I hear it, instantly, I think of grandma. I recall a time when her and grandpa lived on Mount Vernon road, in Cedar Rapids, she had a of pair of doves living in her eave spout, off the roof. We sat on the back porch and she echoed the dove and new which one was the momma. She said to me, "Did you know that doves always live in pairs?" It was the few word conversations that I remember the most. Knowing the significance of the dove, the sound remains a remembrance of her and her gentleness to me. Being as one with the Lord, she is now in his presence.

In the fall of 2000 while grandma was at college, she wrote a piece about the dove, and it is truly an "echo" of her spirit.

"A Symbol"

The dove, a symbol of peace to many

To me the dove speaks of gentleness, innocence and love. The coo, a soft, murmuring sound, gently and lovingly suggesting, "delight". The native Americans believe when you are sad or lonely, to hear that "coo" reassures you, Your kin somewhere, is sending a message of love and remembrance. Coo means (echoic) the nature of an echo. The doves' coo, when I hear it reminds me of a kindred spirit many miles away and brings us close!!!"

What did grandma teach me? There is more to life than television and work. "Read the Word Joel, all the answers you need are right there in it. Appreciate the beauty in the rainbow, trees, stars, and investigate these symbols, and understand why they are there Don't hurry and stress yourself, it will kill you."

So I guess I have learned to appreciate the little things, the clouds, laughter, and the blessings God has bestowed upon me. It was her guidance that slowly molded me and instilled an appreciation of everything life has to offer especially in the worst of times. Even if I didn't realize it yet. For everything I encountered with her, she had an explanation or an answer. She taught me to listen to people and to cherish the time I have with them, especially my children.

I have absolutely loved being a mother, but I haven't done it on my own. She, as my elder, taught me the tools to embrace whatever comes my way. Whether it be good or bad. I can hear her say to me: "Take a deep breath Joel, cry if you need to, and then lets pray. Give it up to the Lord. Don't let your spirit stew!"

So now I am trying to let go of things and leave the worrying to God. I am still trying to practice, but I am human, and with that comes, picking myself up and trying again. Now, at thirty-seven, I am trying hard to practice self discipline in my faith. I read each day and really try to grasp what the scriptures are teaching me. Just as grandma did, I now ask myself, Who will I be? The question coming from an excerpt of grandma's writings:

"Traveling Together"

The thirst persists. Who will I be? To be is to continue "being" in reality. My only real reference book is the scripture. So permit me to share with you. That they should seek the Lord, haply they might feel after him, and find him, though he be not far from every one of us: For in him we live, and move, and have our being; as certain also of your own poets have said, For we are also his offspring. (Acts 17:27-28)

She has taught me to try and live more like the Lord, as we are his children.

She also taught me in the light of (1 Timothy 6:20-21). God's plan upon this earth is nothing new. It is ever continuing, and she urged me to explore and discover what is out there. She sparked that motivation in me in my childhood. The thought of not having that, as a God given, thing would leave me feeling lost in this world. All the things of nature and otherwise, she insisted were right there in the scriptures, and you must discover that in your growth and maturing.

In all the storms that I faced she would guide me and gently calm my spirit. As she says in this July, 2000 letter:

"Yours and my words poured out. And I know the storm is past. So wonderful that God provided the officer friend. God plans way ahead for us believers in him. The Lord says, no weapon that is formed against thee shall prosper; and every tongue that shall rise against thee in judgment thou shalt condemn. This is the heritage of the servants of the Lord, and their righteousness is of me, saith the Lord.(Isaiah 54:17)

She always reminded me that I would come through my tribulations, and she truly did her job as my elder and grandmother. She never left me until she knew I had overcome each storm whether by phone or letter.

The only thing that truly bothered us was not being able to see each other.

(Dear Joel,

Thoughts of you like sparkling dew drops fall gently on my spirit. Strengthening, inspiring, and motivating. I love those honey filled moments. There is an overwhelming desire to make a journey, but no it's not the time. So I wait and grow as I know you are. So come close dear granddaughter, Joel Marie, grasp my heart again and again, as the days fly swiftly by. Joel Marie, a little face, sweet eyes of blue, have followed me the years, so true. Our hearts entwined, our spirits kin. Anticipating each sigh and fear, we mingled such sweet tears, growing together, age and youth, the whole complete. My love abides here Joel, in Jesus, be strong dear one. I know you will, with him you can't go wrong.)

Our spirits understood the beauty of birds, knowing that God created them all. We shared a love for them, especially tuning in to their different and distinct callings, as well as the beauty and the art of flight. I, too, love to fly and enjoy every plane ride I take. She sent me a card which has a firebird on it, and the color of it catches her eye as she describes it to me. I love it.

"Joel, the intenseness of this color fills my spirit with thoughts of you! God clothed this bird with brilliance, and he has been called a firebird. He moves cautiously and slowly, and goes about unnoticed. To me your quietness and intenseness, sound like a paradox? No, You know where you are going and abiding in Jesus, giving you quietness. Your vision of rightness gives the intenseness (red), yet keeping the position of humbleness of mind. There I said it. I love you granddaughter. Thank you for anticipating all the things that bring me joy."

When grandma completed her college courses at Cochise college, in Benson, Arizona where they lived, she felt an emptiness that sort of overwhelmed her. She truly enjoyed the classes and was anxious to do it again. December 10, 2000 she wrote to me with this feeling in her heart: "Joel, I'm lonely right now, I guess it is just a 'let down feeling.' No classes to prepare for. Oh, I have several projects and studies to get into and there is Christmas! Joel, I need to see your face, bear with me, this will pass. Sadness, but tears won't come. They just stick there and ache in my heart. You always know just what to say to give my heart ease. You know the tidbit about sausages and 'girl' talk."

This was something that grandma and I shared when she was here in Cedar Rapids, and I'm sure many of us in the family experienced this. I would stop in the morning before going off to work. First we had a breakfast prayer to carry us through and bless our day. Perhaps a verse or chapter from the Bible. Along with our devotion she would make little sausage links and perhaps some juice and toast. My ultimate favorite, and that of my cousin Tabbitha, was the baked eggs in bread with a strip of bacon or sausage, made in a muffin pan. This unique little breakfast treat was delicious along with the quiet fellowship. I think I remember her saying uncle Ben liked them as well. Then our thoughts poured out to one another and a few laughs to keep things light and real. Then the goodbye hug that sent you on your way in security. No one left her house with out a hug or kiss!

We both missed that terribly after her and grandpa moved to Arizona. That is what she meant by the "girl talk".

She absolutely loved the dry air in Arizona and the beauty, but every now and then she would mention how she missed the change of the seasons and the "green" of the Midwest. She once said to me, "My heart is in Iowa." So I tried to call as often as possible to talk with her, especially when I got her letters of yearning for Iowa.

I know it takes a special someone to love Iowa, and grandma was one of those few. Don't get me wrong. She loved the beauty of all the land, but her spirit always reflected the heartland. She loved the change of the seasons. For a time each was enjoyed. Then the anticipation of the new season brought change that even I felt was an inviting renewal.

In May of 2001 grandma and grandpa came back to Iowa to see everyone for a bit. When they left it was hard to see them go, but a letter to me a week later reflected her heart felt feelings, and the strength the Lord gives when the agony of absence overwhelms one's soul.

(My dearest Granddaughter,

The hour came when our sojourn in blessed Cedar Rapids, so longed for and anticipated was swallowed up; time, seconds, minutes, hours. Our loved ones, the embraces, serious talks, faces engraved on my heart. Then leaving you! Yet cleaving to you, then the tears and the agony of parting. But we are strong in the Lord, and the power of his might holds us both, all of us at home in "his" heart.

Our stay at our son Bill's was wonderful, talking into the night. We learned many things in Bill's heart that he shared. Then in Missouri, my precious Rose, and sweet time with the family. Now the hour for parting has arrived. When you get this letter we should be home.)

Grandma and grandpa were back in Arizona only two months when I had to make the most agonizing phone call of my life. My dad came to my house at 9:30 p.m. on August 29th. Earlier in the evening, I had been lying flat on my back in the living room after working out, when tears started running down my cheeks, and I didn't know why. A unsettling feeling came over me. "What is it Lord?" I remember asking that to this day!

Dad knocked on the window in the kitchen as always. When I let him in I saw an expression of heaviness in his precious blue eyes, one I will never forget. I thought perhaps he needed something to eat. His face so white and his words with soft authority, "Sit down, I need to tell you something." I knew something was awfully wrong. With a quiet, shaking, whispering voice he said, "Jenny died today." I, out of disbelief, said, "Our Jenny, my sister?" Dad and I sobbed, weeping was all I had to offer, and I held him. I felt my daddy's agony and I grew numb and my heart fell into the depths of despair. Oh dear Lord, I'm suppose to go before her! Jenny only 27, I thirty-one. I always thought that was the way it would be. I never thought I would ever be burying my little sister. My thoughts screamed, "My God, My God."

My mind then turned to the weary thought of making the call to grandma. Oh I had to hear her voice as hard as it would be to tell her. I needed her to tell me it's going to be alright! When she picked up the phone I couldn't hardly keep myself from sobbing, I nearly choked on my tears. She heard my sorrow and in a quiet voice asked, "What is it Joel?" With trembling in my voice I told her Jenny had died. She said, "What? Well what do you mean Joel? Jenny Lynn? What happened?"

As I tried not to cry, I whimpered, "An autopsy is being done. After school, Jordan tried to wake her while she was napping, she didn't wake up." Jordan being Jenny's son.

Then I heard a child like voice, quietly moan, "Oh Joel" then her heavy sobs.

I said, "Grandma can you come? I need you."

The heavy darkness that fell upon me was to overwhelming. This was to much, I was weak and could find no strength. Then she promised it would be worked out. Then we prayed for relief of our sorrow, and then she spoke to my dad. Before letting me go, she insisted that I get my feelings out, write them down as I went along, for some relief. After hanging up the phone I was drowning in loneliness.

As she promised, they came. Grandpa, my sweet grandfather, gave her funeral service. At times, himself sobbing. It was hard, but both were extremely loving and carried us through.

These are the times when everything grandma taught me about my faith have to be utilized, and prayer is sufficient. Having family near filled the void and eased the anguish we all felt. We must not forget our family or take it for granted! We have blessed hope that one day we will be with Jenny Lynn, and everyone that goes home to be with Jesus.

When I was in junior high, our class read the book, *The Outsiders.* My best friend Denise and I loved it. Then about a year later they came out with the movie based on the book. In it there was a poem, "Nothing Gold Can Stay". I cherish it. I recalled it and felt it was just right for Jenny. In honor of her, I read it at her funeral. All the while on the inside I was trying to cope with the fact that her life had ended, but the world continued on. I wanted to scream to all, "Stop, don't you see my sister is gone."

Later in December, a few months after Jenny died, grandma was continuing to give me gentle support at those moments when the reality of her death still overwhelmed me. She sent me a very touching letter that had many connecting factors to this poem between our entwined spirits. I had no idea she would see *"The Outsiders"* as I did.

"Joel, Knowing that we both see the same sun in the morning and the same moon at night, makes me feel a little closer to you. My heart was and is deeply moved by the sound of your voice at the church when Jenny passed. The pressure, the pain, the hope and desire for relief from a cloud of darkness, hovering over you. Then with a tear in your voice you say, this came to me to finish. "When I step out into the bright sunlight the shadows dissolve, my sight is clear. Phantoms of anxiety, dread and fear strive to maintain their fake right. Then my Jesus, the Son, draws very near. His rays of light dispel all fear. His peace reigns, my heart is free. An altar offered in praise to his sacrifice on the tree. Now, I'm family, no longer outside. Enfolded in his love, I now abide!"

She continues to write, "Joel, Thank God for Jesus. His holy spirit anchors us and we are safe. Study in the spirit. What is hidden here? Oh my dearest grandchild, thank you! I had written these words down the night before. Nothing gold can stay. Saying to myself, in the spirit, I must get Robert Frost's poem and really look into it. By the way, did you ever see the movie, *"The Outsiders?"* The boy in it quoted it. Isn't it wonderful? Our spirits seized these words to see! How shall we begin? Holy spirit open this to our understanding. First I moved to the 'Strong' concordance and oh the gold! But first let us see, feel and understand the essence of the words. My heart (my spirit) says, "Hush now. The dawn of creation. The green is gold. All shimmering in its pureness. God's early leafs, a flower. The flower of innocence, Adam and Eve. But only so an hour (short time in Eden). Then leaf subsides (Eve), look up the word subside, it means (settles down or sink to the bottom. To leaf (Adam), so Eden sank to grief, The Fall and it's consequence because of the enemy, Satan and the choice Adam and Eve made. Dear God! But God is pure gold. He has a plan of love and compassion. His lamb, Jesus 'Pure Gold' consented to be sin, (2 Corinthians 5:21) or fools gold tainted and bare it on the tree in his flesh (pure gold) took our sin, nailed to the cross that we might be again, pure gold in him, Jesus, as at the first green gold. So dawn goes down to day or sinks down, thus nothing (real) gold can stay. Oh Joel, don't you just love Jesus? Also darling, it tells me, we're young, in a sense, a green, gold shining in our innocence. Then years bring old and knowledge of unholy, but in Jesus we can be gold. So let's proclaim the God of Israel of gold. Oh praise him.

Love in Jesus, dear one! Grandmere."

This truly amazed me. Something I cherished from my childhood could some day be used in sorrow, to comfort my grandmother, and spark such a wonderful study in her, and still bring out joy to us both in the end. This poem is so beautiful to both of us, we seem again to be such kindred spirits even so far apart. A real understanding of something with substance to the soul.

Now I wish to give you Robert Frost's poem to savor, in a new light! It has served its purpose many times in my life, and now I know why God placed it in my heart at the age of thirteen. It has brought peace into my life, as well as my sweet grandmother's, who always went deeper into words to hear what they are really saying to us all!

"Nothing Gold Can Stay"
Nature's first green is gold ,
Her hardest hue to hold.
Her early leaf's a flower;
But only so an hour.
Then leaf subsides to leaf,
So Eden sank to grief.

So dawn goes down to day,
Nothing gold can stay.

All those years grandma was a teacher to me. An encyclopedia-dictionary of the real world and of my precious Bible! It is extremely hard to imagine all this time growing and learning without her. Her studies were deeply enriched. Her guidance gentle, yet firm. Even in her sorrow there was knowledge! If she didn't know it, she would find it. That is what God intended! (Proverbs 2:6) For the Lord giveth wisdom: out of his mouth cometh knowledge and understanding.

We are not to lean to our own understanding, but to his and trust in him with all our heart. (Proverbs 3:5)

January 4, 2002 she wrote:

"It is January 4th, just 224 days until my 80th birthday. The days are dwindling down to a precious few. A new decade coming up. I'm sure it is going to be super blessed, one way or another. Well dear one for the first time I tell you this year, I love you. Sometimes dear one, I just wish you could smooth my hair and tell me again and again, I'm your grand mere! It's a sunny, bright, and golden day with intermittent, darkening clouds. Kind of like life, right? Although the Son, is always there, here. The prince of darkness can be all around, but Jesus the Prince of Light is in me, bringing a brightness and a lifting up."

Her words linger in my spirit each day. If I don't think I can make it through the day I often reflect on her words and of course one of my favorite scriptures from the Bible: "I can do all things through Christ which strengthen me." (Philippians 4:13) Her words have always been more precious to me then material things. December of 2002 she showed this to me once again and reminded me that we should give of ourselves and that material things should not be our priority.

Joel M. Mulholland

"My dearest Jesus and loved ones, this Christmas I give you me."

On this next page, another prayer for her whole family to be stored in heaven. She always poured her heart out for "each" one of us.

December 9th, 2002

"Jesus, in thee I've come to be, a walking, talking, doing prayer. With faltering steps and snow white hair. My heart is fixed ; it rests in thee. My treasures? Loved ones. All around. Precious jewels near and far. In beauty and substance they abound! My children, our own, the grand and great. Given to love and appreciate. Each given a light, coming into the world, a soul to be nurtured and guided in love. An heritage of God to parents unsoiled, his gift unfurled. Please look up the meaning of unfurled in the dictionary. Love in Jesus, Grandma Darlene."

Grandma loved her kindred, as she would say, unconditionally in Jesus.

Grandma and I loved to reflect. I loved to hear her tell me things of the past, a time that captured my imagination. I could fall right into history. She had a wonderful way of describing it and bringing it forth into the present. July 29th, 2003 she does this in regards to my daddy. "This is a special day to write to you in my blessed, sweet, hallowed corner. Sitting at my altar table, praying, thinking and blessing. It is your dad's fifty-fourth birthday, 18 days until my birthday. Your grandma was going on twenty-seven when your daddy was born. Ponder that for a second. We lived in an apartment, owned by Bessie and Arthur Wilcox, off of 8th Ave SE, there in Cedar Rapids. Your first uncle was five, and Bill was two. Again we were attending the Free Methodist church on G avenue at the time and Pastor Olson visited me and Dan at the hospital. From this blessed son, came many blessings, including the precious encourager and

94

comforter, that you, Joel, are to me, as we joy in the Word of God. Oh what a way Jesus had led me. How he has saved me in his precious blood, cleansing. His Holy Spirit given to teach, guide and comfort me. There were also times when I needed reproof and chastising. Thank God I learned, in this he truly loves me. Giving me a heart to receive it and grow in grace. We talk it over now, praise Jesus, but a day is coming of peace and tribulation."

My bond with my grandmother is unbreakable. We have shared so many moments, so many things, and whenever separated we took note and reflected on it and always seemed to come together again. In this particular letter, she is going back over our special moments together, and it is a real true statement that we never really are apart, only in body.

August 13, 2004:

(Granddaughter of my heart,

Joel, In the cool, fresh wind of the Holy Spirit, as I sit at my altar table, yes I am thinking of you. Your life and mine. You are thirty-four soon to be thirty-five. It occurred to me, I was forty-eight when you came to us, your daddy and momma. And all of us. Now my eyes gaze long in the spirit and I see our life, you and me, grandmother and granddaughter together. Your babyhood, so sweet and special. Then a toddler, you at three and me at fifty-one. Our walks in the park below Vivian's, the Holy Spirit touching your little hands. I see them outstretched as you stand on that stump and say, "praise the Lord," then years moving on and the letters you have wrote. I love these letters, and it is hard for me to let them go. Our separation always difficult, but our hearts always intertwined. Then we came back for awhile and a house on eighth avenue and our grown up fellowship. Then my dear one, a married woman , babies, and oh, how you would stop at our front door and joy always entered with you. Then of course another move to Arizona. You're here in my heart, you nourish and bless my life. Your latest for my birthday. Interesting! Very interesting. Your blessed words, "I love you grandma." A wonderful birthday! Yes, I am now eighty-two. I'm so glad, that you are glad I am your grandmother. Then your interesting little phrase, much like my feeling! "I find it hard to share you though." Joel, Neshume-le, which means beloved little soul. Oh the joy of hugging, heart to heart. First God and his son with the Holy Spirit helping. Then your mate, your husband , children and grandchildren! I read this again from a book and I knew. Do you remember the little sweet box you gave me? It says, on the front, "God is watching over you because I asked him to." It's such a lovely, fragile square, china box. So! The spirit whispered, that's it. "Neshume-le." Addressing me now! That's it. I never quite knew what to entrust within this little box. Then just last week, mind you, I knew! It's your treasure, spice box. In it is leaves and cinnamon. And oh Joel, when I open it; the scent of Jesus comes through. Praise him! In special moments of blessing from you, I open it and you're there, dear heart, with me. It will be yours again someday down the road, ours together dear granddaughter Joel.

Love abides, always!
Grandma Darlene.)

I wouldn't call it motivation, but more like spiritual guidance. If we truly go to our elders and look to them for help and understanding, the weight of the world is lifted and many times grandma's words, and the Bible with prayer, have walked me right through the "I don't think I can do this.

September 13, 2004 she sent me this card with the words, "I'm thinking of you!" Then she makes a circle out of her words on the inside of the card. Her own special way of making things more fun. "And Joel, that love filling comes from our precious Jesus and there is a special "thoughts" compartment that causes me to hear your unique little chuckle and laugh. When I think of your satisfaction and pleasure in order and cleanliness, I think of my thankfulness and praise to God in giving you to me to nourish and bless my life. Your intimate heart to heart talks and listening to Jesus. Your love and appreciation of beauty everywhere, your reaching out to all. My wonder that you don't open my letters and cards immediately, but I understand it. The broken little sigh when you need the strength of prayer. Your face and blue eyes, your faithfulness. Your baking bread and cookies, I can see you! The love and joy in your voice when you speak of your husband Kevin and your boys. Hey! I could go on and on because near Jesus you hover in my thoughts, always."

You see by the time I was done reading a letter or card from grandma, I felt like a whole new person, renewed! Then the little love gifts she would send. Sometimes a poem, pictures, sometimes a small book of encouragement or a trinket from years gone by. It all lifted my spirit, gave me strength and made me go forward, and as she always said, "In Jesus." Always hovering over me with guidance. Again more precious then jewels.

When I would talk to grandma, especially as she grew older, she would speak of her day and its events. It always began at the edge of her bed. She spoke of that often. She often would journal at the edge of her bed, and I know as her days came closer to the last, each day became a more needing of her Jesus. She writes one Sunday in 2004,

"Oh! How good to sit in his presence on the edge of my bed. Almost wish I could stay all day. Lord Jesus, umpire my thoughts. Search me, Oh God and know my heart. Try me and know my thoughts and see if there be any wicked way in me, and lead me in the way everlasting.."

So I took these little pieces she would refer to, this one, of course from Psalm 139, and try to use them in my own life. Not perfection, but a way to make my ways better. Our hearts always intertwined. I miss her in the flesh, but I see her in my inner eye and miss her less. For truly in Jesus, we are together, truly kindred spirits! So in closing of this precious chapter, I give you a piece I wrote for grandma reflecting on our days together:

"At The Edge of My Bed"

As I sit at the edge of my bed,
I see the moments of my life.
So clearly, my time aging,
Memories so young.
Just yesterday,
I thought of you, dearly.
Me as a child, the sun in the day,
You as an elder, the hours pass away.
Distinguished rings of a tree,
But with branches that shade.
That sweet fresh feeling,
That time has made.
Through those bitter storms,
You've weathered well.
Like your swift mind,
And the stories you tell.
Beautiful, I to you,
And you to me.
As I sit at the edge of my bed,
It's all very clear to me, you are free!

Chapter 8
(Psalm 90:12 So teach us to number our days, that we may apply our hearts unto wisdom)

Grandma was great at counting the days to her birthday, even from the beginning of the year. Note her birthday was August 16ᵗʰ.

She sent me a letter in 2001 and was pondering the rain as well as her number of days. Uncle Ben & aunt Karen had sent her some stationary that she loved.

"Joel, dear one, isn't this paper unique? Ben and Karen sent it to me for Christmas. Bless them. It is small, but will encourage me to be brief! Ha! Do you think that is possible? I'm sitting here listening to the rain , this is the Sabbath, to me a delight. The sky is a deep purple and blue, now there is this gentle rain. If you were sitting here too, it would be just right to you. No, don't feel sad, oh yes you can. It's good to have these precious moments, and as you say, we are sharing, even now, just delayed a few hours. There was the deep purple sky , then it began to cry. Tears, raindrops, making fertile my heart, and there will be fruit. Our Jesus, God's "one", anointed, born of his love for us. Sheltered, we are in the arms of Jesus. Oh, I love him, don't you? Already the first month of 2001. It is almost a memory. I counted or numbered my days until my seventy-ninth birthday and they are two hundred and one. Glory be, days to apply my heart unto wisdom (Jesus). How I love his word."

"The sun is shining through! Praise our Son of God, the Lord Jesus. Let the peace of God rule in your heart my precious granddaughter. Let His (Jesus) words dwell in you richly, and let your speech be always with grace, seasoned with salt. Well I'm reaching the bottom of my page, so I must measure the thoughts. Isn't our God wonderful, answering, knowing what he is going to do before we ask? Must come to a sweet close here. I'm working and being blessed by your box of love. Most lovingly, grand mere Darlene. That is one thing I always loved to do for my grandma. Shop for things she loved, put them all in a box, and send it to her when she least expected it. It overjoyed me to hear her excitement and appreciation of each item."

In January 2005, an undeniable knowing began to come over me. A real urgency, to pursue. I began to ask grandma questions for which I had no answers. Her thoughts on her children and grandchildren, thoughts on her momma, etc. Then I came across a reflections book that had general questions that you don't always think about. It was published by Hallmark, a journal of sorts. So I sent it to her and asked her to fill it out for me. I thought it would occupy some time as well. It was probably around March that I started to get a sense that grandma wasn't quite as strong as she had been in the past. Letters became fewer, and I was calling her more often. She was sending me things that she wanted me to have. I knew they were very dear to her. Sometime in April, she started to have a hard time breathing. I was extremely concerned. Knowing her thoughts and prayers were in and on Jesus eased my mind. I believe it began around April the 21st. She journals, "Sleeping yet a little. Thank you Jesus. It's 7:25 a.m., I get up and Gerald is right behind. Right to my birdies (Dolly and Jerry) cleaned thoroughly, their home in front of the big window. Cleaned and swept up seeds. Then I gave them more food and water. Then I swept the floor under the garbage can and rug. Now, all is clean for them. Thank you Jesus for giving me this task. I then wash up myself. It is now only 8:15, so I stripped the bed. Oh Jesus I need more breath, help me. And he is. Gerald is entreating, gentle and kind. Bless him. Gerald made his coffee, and we will soon have communion. The communion sweet and peace reigns. Thank you Jesus for helping me breathe. Then I move on to clean and rid myself of all excess paper on my altar table. Now almost noon, Praise God! I fixed two basted eggs and a bran muffin. The phone rang, it is our precious Rose. I was just thinking and pondering about her. Then she calls. I related the story of our gift, Dolly and Jerry our birds. She was pleased. Touch her hip and heal it, in Jesus name. I believe it Jesus. Bless her Jesus. How I love her. Goodbye dear one. The rest of the day the air is heavy with moisture. The air is weighty and oppressive. Lighten O' Lord , the air, in Jesus name."

" Gerald went to get the mail. A precious, joyful, blessed letter from Dan. Thank you Jesus. I have a card and letter, I want to write to Dan. Thank you for this son, dear Jesus, and I want to get a note to Rose, dear Rose. I tried to call Redemption Church in Cedar Rapids twice. I thought Dan might be there, but no answer. Lord help me, contain my desire to communicate with your servant, my son, just now. Praise Jesus. It is all in your hands. Oh Jesus, air is so heavy!"

" Joel called, we talked of many things concerning what's in my reflections book that contains all she desires to know. Bless her heart. Also we talked of lilacs and their scent and how they embody so many memories! Thank you for Joel. Yes Lord! Thank you. Then she had to go, first talking to dad, bless them Jesus." Then I returned to my relaxing chair. Then finally Gerald found a show. *Sundowner*'s. It is an Australian environment, sheep country. It was wonderful to watch them sheer the sheep and as it says in the scripture. (Isaiah 53:7) He was oppressed and he was afflicted, yet he opened not his mouth. He is brought as a lamb to the slaughter and as a sheep before her sheerer is dumb, so he openeth not his mouth. Wonderful, and as I looked at the terror stricken eyes of that sheep, yet no sound, I saw Jesus eyes on the cross."

" Then after *Sundowner's*, off to bed to read 'The Must of Love'. My son caused me to think of it when I said, 'I love you.'

His answer, "You have to."

Grandma responded, "Yes, that is the 'must' of love. God is love! He must love his creation and grace weeps when that love is rejected."

"April 22nd, Friday 2005. Day of preparation! Lovely, blessed day, reading the precious word. Yes, I desire to be a keeper at home. Good and discreet, yes and obedient to my own husband, according to his will. He is first, preeminent, in my heart. (Titus 2:5) So to the tasks before me. Out to the kitchen, Gerald already took cover off Dolly and Jerry, they are talking and chattering. Gerald likes to talk to them and so do I. I cleaned the floor and table as well as the bottom of their cage. Then I went and cleansed myself. Thinking of fixing rice and cranberries for when Gerald comes in from cleaning out the car. Fixed it, then off to get dressed then catch up on my journal. I straightened the bed sheet and quilt. Then freshened them. All accomplished. We ate our rice and cranberries. Heated it up, very good. Bed smoothed out for fresh air. You are helping me Lord. By the way, must means to be allowed to, have to, commanded or requested to, urged to. Anyway, Gerald finished his rice and cranberries, ought to hold him for awhile, he is going back out to finish cleaning Betsy, the van. I am relaxing now for awhile at my altar table. Reading my reflections, must finish for Joel. So I have been reflecting on my life for the last hour and a half and it is now 3:20 p.m. I called my son Dan, praying that he would be there! I waited expectantly, he answered quietly. I said, "Thank you Jesus. Then an explosion of praise and glory as we prayed and agreed the agreement of prayer for my need. I talked with Gerald of Dan, and our victory prayer, and Dan's love to him, dad. Began to make tuna salad for sandwiches and rice a roni. We ate. Dear God help me, then the news, washed up, then ready to rest, Dear Jesus!"

"Saturday, Sabbath delight, April 23rd. It is getting lighter, Oh my healer Jesus, help. I don't mind, even welcome walking through the valley of the shadow of death, holding your hand, fearing no evil. Jesus, only you breathe me through. Thank you."

"We partook of communion, blessed body and blood of Jesus. And sitting in the sun I receive healing, in his body and blood. I must take it easy and slow though, I realize. I called Stephen and asked for his blessed prayer of faith. He is very concerned. I promised him I would get medical attention if it was necessary, but I am trusting Jesus! All the way. Bless him, he prayed for his (momma), and I prayed too. I told him that dad was right here watching over me. So be it, peace! A little later Marty called. I assured her it is better, she is very concerned. Don't, I prayed, lets trust Jesus, she prayed for me as well. Bless her!"

Marty is my uncle Steve's wife. Grandma told me that she is just like another daughter to her. At this point we were all trusting in Jesus to protect grandma, but on alert as to what she may be needing medically.

She writes, "I laid out the tasks for dad to do. Empty the garbage, put a new bag in, wash trays, tasks finished. Good boy!!! We still need to put washing in the dryer. Gerald left to go to the store, mail daughter Rose's card and pick up our mail. It is now 12:25 in the afternoon, I tried to call Daniel again, but he is not at the church. Bless him Jesus. Then later I called Joel just to run over what Jesus has done for me this morning, bless and keep her, dear Jesus! Going to rest now like a good girl."

"Resting, resting, resting, now 12:35 and phone rings. It is Mart, she is home now, asked how I am. I am much better honey, Jesus bruised Satan under my feet. He can't get to my chest, praise Jesus! I love Mart dearly. I spoke to Stephen letting him know, I'm better now honey, Jesus is helping me breathe. They are going to call later, dear Jesus."

"It is now almost 1p.m. Gerald is home. Checked groceries, he got two more items than I had down, oh well. Dear Jesus help me! Gerald fixed three pouched eggs, and some bread with a fourth of a banana. I ate most of it and very thankful. Trying to be agreeable and not irritate Gerald, and he's trying to help me. So we are bearing and forbearing as the scripture says. At 2 p.m. Gerald invited me to the patio to listen to the thunder and rain. Wow! I just found a scripture, a word for me. What my heart cried this morning. Thou hast heard my voice! Hide not thine ear at my breathing, at my cry. Thou drewest near in the day that I called upon thee, thou saidst, fear not. (Lamentations 3:56-57) Oh how timely and fitting for my ordeal and trial, this very morning! In my breathing difficulty, how I love your word Jesus."

"Later I sit in the chair in the living room, just resting. It has been thundering and a little rain coming down. Oh, how fragrant! The scent of the earth, the green trees really pronouncing it's spring! Finished studying the Sunday class portion. Now I will try to take a bath, help me Jesus. What wonderful help and support, holding of my hand, Jesus and my dear husband, Gerald. Then the phone rang. Gerald answered it. It was Joel. She said she would call back in twenty minutes. When I got out of the tub the phone rang again. Oh, it's my dear Stephen. He asks, "How are you momma?"

I respond, "I am just out of the hot tub Stephen and I feel real good. Dad stayed close by if I needed him.

"Rest momma." His gentle reply.

"I did, dear one, all afternoon. It is so good to sense your love. I love you Stephen." Then Mart came on. I said to her, It is so good to know you are loved. Bless you. Do you work tomorrow? She replies, 'No.' Good then you too, can rest. Mart ends with, 'We will call you tomorrow. You stay home and rest.' I tell her, honey I am, bless you. Then back to Stephen, 'Goodnight momma, I love you.' I tell him, I love you Stephen and I feel your arm around me."

"Gerald and I watched the 1994 Billy Graham service until 7:30. Joel hasn't called back. She must be tending to Ben, Dan and Colin. Bless her Jesus. At ten 'til eight Joel called as she said she would. She has been praying for me all day. Bless her precious heart. "I'm fine." I told her, after my bath and everyone has showered me with love and prayers. Stephen and Mart called me five times, bless them."

"Joel had a yard sale with some neighbors on the block, her and Kevin made $120.00. Praise the Lord! Love between us is so sweet and dear. Brings my Jesus ever so near. She prayed again for me, bless her. Gerald and I watched, *The Little Colonel*, a sweet, clean, Shirley Temple movie. There are some clean things left in this world. It is now 10:30 p.m. help me Jesus as I lay down. Goodnight my dear Jesus."

The last thing in this sweet, little journal, said: April 24, 1st day, Sunday 2005. I'm sure grandma had every intention of filling this out, but she didn't get the chance to finish writing because grandpa took her to the hospital that morning. He called me about 10 a.m. and said that grandma was having trouble breathing. He took her to Benson hospital. When he got her there the medical help realized she needed greater medical attention then they could give. So they flew her, by helicopter, to Tucson Medical Center where they immediately began to monitor her heart. She still had the bronchial infection and her heart rate was not staying consistent. It was continually up and down.

The morning of the 24th was extremely hard for me. I knew from the way she had talked all week that something was definitely wrong. I tried to call aunt Becky and alert her, but I couldn't get through. So I sent her an email to call me immediately.

I was in the midst of the final day of the yard sale and couldn't keep my mind off grandma. I prayed, "Lord, please keep her in your hands." After a couple of hours Becky called. I explained that grandpa had taken her to the hospital. Of course she became very concerned for grandma.

Later I began to pull out the writings that grandma had sent to me over time. I laid them out, putting them in order by dates. Two weeks earlier we had discussed her thoughts about all of her children. I expressed to her that I would like to have her thoughts now, in 2005, about all seven of her children. She said, "I will send you that plus two writings from 1969 and 1971."

I was really excited when I received them this week I began to organize all the writings she had sent to me, preparing for our book.

I sat there at the kitchen table and read through them, hot tears began to roll down my cheeks. I couldn't move, I just froze. I could no longer hold back. The dearest person to me was on the edge of life, struggling for breath, and I couldn't touch her precious hand to comfort her. The deafening silence of the phone and the quiet around me engulfed me, and time stood still. I began to pray and quietly whisper, "Oh Jesus, please have mercy. Jesus, Jesus, hear me now." Nothing else would come. I looked out the window and peered around at the green of the grass and trees, the colors poured over my spirit and paralyzed my eyes. The birds she so loved, continued to chirp and life continued on and minutes seemed to linger in my mind.

I had booked tickets for May 24th to fly to Arizona to see her. It was to be a surprise gift to her. Grandpa and cousin Jennifer would pick me up at the airport. Now I began to question whether I should wait that long. I didn't know what to do.

Should I rebook the flight and go now? I thought about it all afternoon. Especially because Friday, when her and I spoke, she said, "If I become real sick I want you here." Should I wait, or will she get better? Strangely enough all three of my boys were really good this day. I needed that. No extra stress. Of course, Colin Ray, in his concerned manner, asked right away if she was ok. I explained that we would have to wait and see, they were on their way to the hospital for treatment and that we should continue to pray for grandma.

I have matured. I can feel it. No panic, just tears and a sense of our great Father close by, speaking the truth fully to my soul. Sensing she knows as well, that I am with her in spirit, praying and knowing her need for prayer this day. We finally shut the yard sale down. It was Sunday and not many were coming. In my eyes Sunday wasn't a day for a sale anyway.

I spoke with my precious, understanding husband and explained my thoughts of going down now. He agreed that it may be best to go now and see her, that way if something would happen to her, that at least I got to see her one last time. No, surely the Lord has more time for her. Oh please, I thought.

The next morning on April 25th I spoke to my boss and he rebooked my flight for me, to leave on April 28th. I asked for my vacation time early, as my anniversary date was June 13th, he agreed. I was extremely grateful.

In the meantime I spoke to my uncle in Arizona to see if I could stay with him in order to be near grandma. I knew she wasn't out of the hospital, but I wasn't taking any chances. She needed me now. I would not ignore my gut feeling.

Many things to take care of before I go. I immediately called my sister in law , Phyllis, to see if she would come and stay with the boys while I was gone. She said she would as long as she didn't have anything else scheduled. I knew they would be in great hands; and I wouldn't have to worry. My boss made the final arrangements for the flight. I got everything taken care of and packed things as the week went along. I bought grandma a new pad and pen. A postal stamp on the pen with a rose on it. I knew she would love it.

In the midst of preparation, a little nervousness came over me. We had people coming out to put new windows in, and I wanted that project to go well, Ben hadn't ever been without me for more then a day or two. Knowing he loved his aunt Phyllis, I didn't have time to dwell on it. He would be in good hands. Then wondering if Kevin would be able to bear the whole load with the boys.

When Thursday finally came, I got up very early. Around four, to get ready. I had to be at the airport by six am. Kevin, my husband, took me out to the airport. Then we said our goodbyes.

After checking my luggage in I waited for a bit. Finally the flight was ready for boarding, I was nervous about going through the Chicago airport, but I absolutely love to fly. The flight took off without any problems, went through Chicago, and finally on into Tucson.

Whenever I come off a flight into a new city, I am always a bit uneasy. I'm not always sure which way to go. As I slowly made my way through the crowd, I found a flight of steps and an escalator. It seemed to be a good choice, so I took the escalator down. I started to peer through all the people. I caught eye of three very familiar faces. Relief began to run all through my body. Of course a cowboy hat that peered over all the heads in the crowd. Ah, there's my precious, beloved grandfather! Seeing him brought a calm, relief over me. I missed him so much! Cousin Jennifer came along and it was great to see her again, we had to catch up. My uncle, at grandpa's side, looked good. I was anxious to know what he had been up to. I moved closer to grandpa, and offered open arms, I wrapped my arms around him. Oh I hugged him so tight. I missed him so much! There was security in his eyes, that it would be alright.

We left the airport and headed for the car. As I peered over the landscape I could see the hazy mountains and desert plants that grandma had described to me. Immediately I could see and feel how arid the desert was. Very desolate between each town as well. The land brown and hard, with no color or grass whatsoever. That I didn't like. No green except for the plants! The barren ground was uncomforting to me.

There were many beautiful cactus plants and flowers. Some I had never seen before. There is one particular one that is a mirror of an aloe plant, but it is definitely a cactus. Each had its own unique character that seemed to be fitting to the landscape.

While we drove through the city I could see a distinct Hispanic and Indian influence to everything, especially in the architecture. The designs of the buildings and the patterns on them, very evident. Pretty in its own unique way.

We headed for the hospital. Grandpa drove, and my uncle David lead the way. As we approached the Tucson hospital, I could see it was more spread out on one floor rather than going upward. I was very anxious to see grandma. We parked and approached the entrance to the hospital. I wanted so badly to run to her room. We finally reached her room, and everyone entered, before me. I came in last, hiding around the corner, just a bit. Grandma said, "Get in here Joel, a little birdie told me you were coming." There was such joy on her face, as there always had been when someone came to greet her. She was sitting up in the chair. I hugged her firm, and she gave out a little "ooh." I apologized. I had forgotten for a moment how fragile she really was. Her voice comforted my inner spirit. "Dear Jesus." I missed her so much I hadn't seen her since 2001. Such a wonderful feeling to touch her hands and hear her precious voice in person. It felt like receiving gold. It went right to my soul to see her hands broke out and so bruised from the needles. Her body weight had dropped dramatically and it was unsettling. My heart heavy laden, reality filled me with sadness. It overwhelmed my spirit for a moment. I had to face the inevitable, her time was at hand. Only God knew when.

It took everything I had, not to break out, in a river of tears. Her inner person was still as alive as ever. Perhaps a little slower, but still my precious grand mere. I didn't want to dwell on the illness because I knew she didn't like that. Grandma spoke for a moment on the events that lead to her being in the hospital. She told me they needed to get her heart rate stabilized.

The nurses, with a quiet authority, told us she needed a lot of rest and wasn't getting it because of all the concerned phone calls from family. About every twenty minutes grandma insisted on having pen and paper. I could see the yearning in her precious, blue eyes. My Lord, she was never without a pen in her hand. Grandpa and I spoke to her. I softly said to her, "Grandma you need to rest for now, and gain strength. In order for you to get better and come home. I knew it was extremely hard for her to just lay there. I thought if this really was her last days, perhaps it wouldn't hurt to let her write a little bit. I told her to rest awhile, and I would try to get her some paper soon. I gently looked into her tired, tender, blue eyes and asked her to listen to the hospital staff taking care of her. It was their job to protect her health. She gave me that look of: "I don't want to, but if I have to I will." A half willed submission. I have seen that look many times. Her nose and eyebrows scrunch up a little. Her eyes roll down a bit with lips pursed, but no words are said in defiance.

Grandma was so use to taking care of herself and others, that it was hard to give that over to someone else. I know this feeling. It is hard to succumb to dependence of others! All these years, cooking, cleaning, laundry, providing for everyone else's needs. To just lay there was not easy for her. She didn't have to say it. I sensed it and could see it in her eyes. This forced me to face the fact that someday I too, will have to look ageing right in the eye and surrender to God. That will be the only way. Any other would make me crazy.

She was receiving so many phone calls that they finally had to put a stop to it for a day or so.

The first night I was there, I really thought she would be out in a few days. However, as the week went on, she began to weaken. Her appetite was diminishing, and she didn't always like what they had on the menu. Grandpa, Jen and I, sat with her at lunch time and made sure she ate some of her lunch. I told her she could order something she liked. She didn't have to go solely by the menu. That seemed to please her a little. So we wrote out or circled what she wanted for each meal.

She asked that I stay with her, but I felt I was keeping her from her needed rest. Then she would say to me, "There are so many pills they want me to take. I don't know why I have to take all of these!" I know she despised it. She always asked the nurse what each one was for before she would take it. The look on her face as if to say, "I'm to old for this, I'm not going to start now." My grandmother was never one for heavy meds, and it was very apparent. I recall at different times she would get a prescription from the doctor and she would tell me, "I didn't even need these I shouldn't have gotten them. The Lord helped me heal."

I tried to encourage her to take the meds to help her get better. Perhaps selfish, I felt it was critical for her in this situation. Even with a short visit, grandma would tire quickly. I encouraged her to rest, and I would tell her we would come back in the morning. She would say to me, "You will come back, won't you?" It resounded and echoed deep in my heart… "Mother is the name of God on the lips of children." I whispered, "Of course I will grandma."

"Can you bring me some paper? No one will give me any paper to write on." Anyone who knows my grandma, knows she was never without a pen in her hand ready to take notes on everything. This went right to my heart! She couldn't let go of her inkhorn. Knowing my grandmother, this was truly her way of relaxing, and it did help her fall asleep.

After some time spent with her I would hug her goodbye. With each departure I couldn't help feeling like I was abandoning her.

I stayed with my aunt and uncle except for the three nights that I spent at grandma and grandpa's. At my aunts request, my cousin Jen and I went to grandma's to clean the house real well and shampoo the carpets. I wanted everything to be nice and clean for grandma.

When I wasn't at the hospital, I spent a little time catching up with grandpa and Jen. We talked about family and how everyone was doing, and how grandma was doing. My aunt kept me posted on her condition when I wasn't at the hospital and encouraged me not to worry. She reassured me grandma would be alright as long as she continued to do what she needed to do to get well.

My aunt is a nurse at Tucson Medical Center, and she had put the order in for grandma to have no more phone calls. She said there were an enormous amount coming in and grandma wasn't resting. Her heart rate would fluctuate out of control, and she had to rest. Her sodium count had escalated, and she had to have the medication to keep the heart rate under control. I heard the critical concern in her voice, and I knew it wasn't the time for her compromise. She did an awesome job of overseeing grandma's care!

At night I would sit outside. The Arizona sky could be seen for miles, and the sunset beamed with reds and orange. In the evening you could see every star in the sky. There wasn't much hindering the view. It was very dry and warm during the day and cool after ten at night.

Grandma sent me a picture a year ago of the sunset in Tucson and said, "Joel, you must come see this beauty." There really is unique of beauty to the sky, along with the Catalina mountains off in the distance.

My aunt was sweet enough to give me their room to stay in. I insisted I could sleep on the floor in the living room, but she wouldn't have it. She fixed up their RV for her and my uncle. I slept very well that first night. The activities of that day, and the trip from home exhausted me. I had gotten up at four and didn't go to bed the first night until almost two a.m. The second day I was up early and anxious to go back to the hospital to see grandma, but I waited on grandpa's word. My aunt asked if Jen and I would go down and clean the house in Benson. We went to see grandma and we told her of our intentions. She was happy to hear it.

As Jen and I sat with grandma, I could see her breathing was heavy and exaggerated, I had never seen her breath like that. She showed us the beautiful plant that aunt Mart and uncle Steve had sent from Iowa. It had gorgeous violet and purple colors. She loved it. Then she looked me straight in the eye, as if to read my thoughts. It caught me off guard, and she whispered to me, "Joel, if I have to go, I am ready. I don't mind one bit. I'm ready to see my Jesus. I love you Joel." I saw the same love and compassion in her precious, blue eyes that captured my heart when I was four or five. Before we left she said with compassion, "On the table, at home there is a little journal with a bear on it. I want you to have it. It will bless you and give you my thoughts in the last few weeks." I knew she was aware that her time was at hand.

I felt tears building. The thought of death scourged my heart with agony, knowing it would come in God's time. But her words seemed to nourish my soul. Her eyes were sunken in a little, with a heavy darkness beneath them, her face was thin and pale, her arms so purple and bruised from the needles, and her body frail, but her words rang strong and honest!

"I love you too, grandma!" That settled my spirit. Even if I had never spoke to her again, I could now go home knowing what she thought at this point and time in her life. I didn't have to ask, God knew what I needed to hear, and she put closure on that matter in my mind and spirit. It would be selfish of me to beg for more time if she didn't want it. God made it possible for me to be at her side and for that I was thankful. I hugged her and assured her I would be back.

Jennifer and I went to Benson. Their house is about thirty miles from Tucson. The scenery on the way was beautiful. We rode through mountain and desert terrain, very much a desert land, cactus and weed like plants everywhere. Jennifer spoke of the necessity of having water in your vehicle in this part of the country in case of a break down, and I could see why. The area was so barren. When we reached Benson, it reminded me of a small, southern town. The house was in a cozy little neighborhood, kind of tucked away. The mountains could be seen behind the homes. In the front yard, no grass, just cactus like plants and a short tree. The house looked like it was made of stucco. The front doorway had a heavy, metal door, unlike the doors in our area.

When we went inside, I could feel my grandma everywhere, that hadn't changed. The place looked pretty good. She had kept insisting that the refrigerator needed to be cleaned out. So I took everything out of the refrigerator and cleaned it real good. We went through the cupboards and threw out the old stuff, and washed the walls, fans, and windows.

Then I tackled the bathroom. I could see as I got further into it that grandma was a little less able to do some things. Her house was always spotless, she insisted on it. When we were finished it was about eleven at night. Time to rest. I slept in the guest bedroom. The bed was hard, but it worked. It seemed much cooler in Benson. But I didn't sleep soundly. Jennifer and I headed back to Tucson the next morning. When we returned, there was still no word on when grandma would be released. Maybe next week.

I spent that weekend talking to grandpa. Grandpa expressed his frustration with the doctors, wanting better answers. My aunt would fill us in daily. She told us the cardiologist would decide on a pacemaker by Wednesday, May fourth.

As the week progressed, I realized grandma wouldn't be released, so I tried to help her concentrate on eating her meals to regain her strength. I tried to help her with the menus, but a lot of it didn't appeal to her. I ordered the items she liked or would eat. She would say, "they are so big;" and would scrunch up her nose, but the portions were small. She was weak and slow at spooning or forking her food. Grandma liked to relax and really enjoy her food. I recall her saying at times to me when we would have dinners, "Don't hurry through your food, relax and enjoy it dear." She savored the tastes and the aromas. I didn't see that now as she struggled to eat and scrunched up her nose. Wednesday the cardiologist came in and spoke to the family. Afterwards, Grandma explained that they would be putting in a pacemaker. She said it would keep the heart rate from going to low, and explained how they would be putting in the pacemaker. She explained how much time it would take, and said it would be a wire running down to the heart. This was to be done on Thursday sometime.

That night, I was going through and straightening my stuff, and my aunt came into the bedroom with a compassionate look in her eyes. As we talked, I just broke down. I had been pretty strong through the whole week, but I felt like I was slowly losing grandma. I felt helpless to help her! My aunt reassured me that the surgery, the medication, and the recovery with rest would help her to get well. We hugged, and I felt so much better. She understood our closeness and understood my uncertainty. She is a very compassionate person. I was thankful for all of her hospitality during my stay. I knew the Lord would help grandma, and my aunt would be there to oversee her care, but in my heart I knew her time was at hand.

I believe it was the day before I left that my cousin Jen wanted to take me up into the mountains. Something good to take back home with me. They were beautiful up close and it was exciting to get up closer to those huge, prickly cactus' and to see their substance. It felt wonderful to be amidst nature's beauty. Grandma and I always shared that, and I had grown to savor those moments. Because you may never get to see that beauty again. I absorbed all the landscape had to offer me. Jen and I had a great time.

At the end of my stay, the last day, I went to see grandma. I walked the hall of the hospital recalling how our moments together in this life had really gone all to fast and I hadn't even noticed until now. I tried with all I had not to break down. An empty feeling ran through me. I walked into the room and her face showed some weakness in spirit. Emotions at the brink of breaking open. I hugged her and ran my hand across her soft, pale cheek. I nearly choked on my tears. My eyes welting and finally overflowing, I couldn't help it. She had been a huge part of my life for thirty-five years and a piece of my life would be barren not hearing her voice. Her words still touch my spirit. "We will see each other again." We talked a bit and hugged. I kissed her on the forehead, and I knew it was time to go. I will never forget the look in her deep, blue eyes when I looked back as I was leaving.

As I walked out of the hospital, I looked up toward the heavens, for I felt an emptiness come over me. Inside I was crying on the Lord's shoulder. Our final separation tore at my soul!

I had said my goodbyes to grandpa and hugged him tightly. "I love you grandpa." I didn't want to leave him either. I could sense the uncertainty in his hug. It was the tightest hug I had ever received from him I thought I saw a tear in his eye as I headed for the door.

It was now time to head for the airport. Jen took me, and I was missing grandma and grandpa already, but I managed to keep my composer. Jen stopped at a shop in the airport and bought me some jelly made from cactus juice, a sweet gift. I believe it was prickly pear. I hugged her firm and headed for my boarding area. There was a few minutes wait, alone, not just myself, but lonely. As I went down that corridor and stepped into, as grandma would say, that big piece of steel, I felt the tears and a huge lump in my throat, burning from holding back, trying to control the emotion, until I got past the pilot and attendant. I knew in my heart this had been the last time I would see my grandmother on this earth. I just knew.

Joel M. Mulholland

The plane started to take off and move down the runway slowly. I tried to keep looking out the window, to hide my emotions. The sound of the engines, the plane lifting, and the plane going higher and higher was a final reminder of leaving grandma. Oh Dear God! The roaring of the engines made me cry. I knew the flight home would be a long one. Flying over the Grand Canyon echoed grandma's appreciation of the earth and what grandma instilled in me as a child. A grand view of existence and making the most out of the one life you have, including Jesus along the way.

When the plane finally touched down in Cedar Rapids, I felt a sense of release as the pressure of the wheels grabbed the ground and pulled me back. As I walked off the plane onto the ground, a little despair lingered. Kevin was waiting for me in the lobby and tears came to my eyes as we hugged and picked up my luggage. I had to shake it off, as the boys would be overjoyed to see me. The ride home would be quiet. A time to concentrate on seeing my three handsome sons.

When I walked out of the airport the brightness of the landscape nearly blinded me, especially the green of the trees and grass. It completely overwhelmed my senses. In that instant it made me appreciate the color we have in the natural scene of our landscape. Very visible in the Midwest. I recall telling grandma this when I spoke to her again after she got home from the hospital. She told me that her heart would always be in Iowa, and she loved the change of the seasons and the natural colors. It is etched in my inner conscienousness. It was the ending of one season, and the renewal of the next that we so enjoyed.

It was a long, silent ride home. Looking away I felt hot tears slip down my cheeks. As Kevin and I drove past the Iowa corn fields, I reflected on my trip and I knew I had made the right choice to go when I did. God had walked me right through all the plans and everything had fallen right into place. No regrets, my mind is at ease.

After grandma had come home from the hospital, I communicated with her by phone for about two weeks, and I received one more letter from her. This was a small, one page note. It said it all, and again, revealed to me that her time was at hand. She was very aware of it being close. She wrote:

"My beloved Joel,

"Rejoice", someday there will be no time, it will be morning!! We will see Jesus precious face, and always it will be morning. Dearest granddaughter, we will see each other always in the morning. Hey! I love you. In my heart your name rings like a melody. I thank you for coming and all you have done. Your blessed husband, his love for you and your sons."

Love,
Grandmere Darlene.

As I look back and reflect on time and how it is truly in God's hands, I see how grandma got a little better, strengthened some, and spoke of her thankfulness for his hand on her.

On June 2nd, grandma and grandpa were staying with my uncle. I called and spoke to her for just a bit. She spoke of trying to finish her reflections book for me. I told her not to worry about that to just get her rest Her voice sounded a little stronger. She reassured me she would not mind being with her Jesus. I didn't talk long. I wanted her to rest and be quiet. I assured her I would call after the weekend and insisted she should be still in Jesus. In my heart I wanted to talk to her and never hang up, but she needed to continue to gain her strength. Oh how I sensed from God this was the last call I would ever make to her when I hung up the phone. No sense in trying to fool myself. The hour was at hand. I could hear silence.

Early in the morning, Saturday, June 4th, the phone rang. I recognized the voice. My uncle asked if I was sitting down. No point in going any further, I thought. She is with Jesus! I couldn't cry, I just listened and received his official word. Then I could only think of my precious grandfather. Strong? Yes, but this was his beautiful bride of 61 years. I asked my uncle David if he was alright, and he assured me he was ok.

Later I spoke with my grandfather about those last few hours, and he had this to say, "She had went to the hospital about four days before she passed, and she said, "I don't want to stay in this hospital tonight." They were staying at Dave and Terri's so Terri could also keep a careful eye on her.

The evening before she died, grandma still had enough strength to put her curlers in her hair. She did this every night for as long as I can remember. She took great pride in how her hair looked. It was so white and soft. When she got down to the last curler, she asked grandpa to come and help her put it in. He told her, "I don't know how to get them things in." So he handed it back to her and somehow she found the strength in her weary arms to put it in. Grandpa recalls her saying, "Jesus, just take me home." Grandpa feels that she died sometime between one and four in the morning. He said, "I got up at four and found her. She looked like she had went to sit down on the edge of the bed and slipped down to the floor, lying down on her side. Her head on her shoulder. My beautiful bride. She now was my heavenly beauty with a peaceful smile. Sad? Yes, but I knew she had to suffer no more. It was overwhelming, so sudden."

Grandpa thought back to the time when he was about to go off to war, her words. "I will be here when you come home." Now it was as if she were to say from heaven, "Now I am here waiting for you to come home!"

So, now I had to reach my daddy. I didn't cry when David told me, but when I reached my daddy, and I heard his voice, all I could get out was "daddy", and the dam broke loose. I was so overwhelmed with tears, my heart fluttered. I think he knew at that point.

In the days to come another trip would be made. My father, brother, aunt Becky, and I made the trip to Arizona to see grandma's body laid to rest. I say this because she wouldn't want me to dwell on death as she associated it with the devil. So I will leave it with scripture as she is now in the presence of Jesus.

1 Corinthians 15:54-58 (So when the corruptible shall have put on incorruption, and this mortal shall have put on immortality, then shall be brought to pass the saying that is written, Death is swallowed up in victory. O death, where is thy sting? O grave, where is thy victory? The sting of death is sin: and the strength of sin is the law. But thanks be to God, which giveth us the victory through our Lord Jesus Christ. Therefore, my beloved brethren, be ye steadfast, unmovable, always abounding in the work of the Lord, forasmuch as ye know that your labor is not in vain in the Lord.)

So it is that her physical body is gone, but she lives in the bosom of Abraham. Amen. I leave this chapter with one last piece that grandma wrote when she was 78. Funny, but I can't help see a bit of Iowa in her thoughts, along with her walk with Jesus.

My Journey

"In the land of Were, Are and Will Be"

My journeys' been a learning tree,
A youthful "blade" he promised me.
He would teach, nurture, and provide.
If I would only walk by his side.
His seed in me, brought forth, the "ear,"
Learning, growing, some days were drear,
Then the day of "full corn" did appear.
When my "fruit" is ripe,
Morning, noon or night.
His gentle sickle will gather home,
Because the harvest time is come.
Darlene M. Long Age 78

Chapter 9
(Proverbs 10:7, The memory of the just is blessed: but the name of the wicked shall rot)

So few souls today, live righteously. Grandma has made that possible for the next generation of her family. I see grandma's beliefs and values in many members of our family. The things we appreciate, the giving, loving and trusting in the Lord for all our needs. We stand our ground in our strong beliefs that we must live the right way. Appreciation for so much around us; from the beauty of nature to the awe of giving birth.

Grandma has touched many lives, some we are not even aware of. She was a person of honor and superior standing. One who's worth brings respect. She has left memories in our hearts like impressions in clay. They were molded, then hardened and can't be removed. Even if it was through tough love. They carry over into our daily lives, brought to mind in each of us in a different way. She was steadfast in the belief that love is needed to survive. It may be differently expressed for others, tho nonetheless true. Love, unselfish, loyal, with benevolent concern for the good of others. She believed the only way to have this is through our Lord, Jesus Christ. Her faith was a "So

123

shine" faith, alive and disciplined as the stars are to the heavens. Never doubting Messiah. A disciple in his word. She tried to guide us all with the same love. She is, and I say, is because she is with us in memory, through the Lord's grace she is in heaven with the Father. She sees and knows His presence even now. She is alive in Christ for eternity.

I open this chapter, with thoughts from others. Family, friends, and acquaintances, thoughts and memories that remain strong and live on in our own lives.

I start with a poem that my aunt Rebecca wrote when she was at Mcpherson College, in Kansas. Grandma sent me this poem on my thirty-first birthday. My sweet aunt makes it very clear how memories stay with us, and it truly blessed me in my time of need.

"Memories!!"

Where can one go to escape memories?
Is there a certain place to hide?
They seek you out, no matter where you are,
Then bring on shouts of joy or sobs of sorrow.
The "joyful" ones are kind to you,
And fill your heart with gladness.
But then, along comes a sorrowful one,
It rips and tears, inside and out.
That's when the sobs begin.
No, memories are here to stay,
There's no where to hide, no place to go.
One thing, only one thing.
Look at it, face it, and say,
Yes, that's my memory, I went through that,
Bear it joyfully or sad.
Look to the new day with hope,
For always there are memories.

Rebecca A. Long

On March 16, 1998, grandma wrote in her journal, on being a mother, it still echoes in my heart.

As mothers, we are never perfect. Mothers are always striving to balance love and discipline; working to get it right, and no one understands until they become a parent.

Her gut feeling on this was very real, and she mothered us all and gave us strength. She writes, "Such a longing! Lord Jesus, How shall I deal with this inner "sob" of my soul? I face the fact, I am a "mother". Yes it's what you made me. With your help, I fulfilled my calling to the best of my ability. Whatever is good, filtered through the maze of my mistakes and is to your glory. I thank and praise you. Today, this spirit has come upon me of love for their souls, and I know you are handling all of that. Do you understand Jesus? My need, just a token, an outward indicator, an expression or divine sign. I leave it in your hands. Comfort me! Please!"

Grandma loved her children dearly. She expressed her thoughts on her children in April, 2005 and what they have become to her. Then along with that I asked each of her children to reflect on what she meant to them.

Grandma wrote on April 5th, 2005 in a letter to me. "You ask, How do I see my children in 2005? So, I see!"

"My son William George, my spring time baby. So dignified, faithful, loving and caring. Still an ambassador for Christ. Everywhere he goes, he works and preaches in the word of God. Oh lord bless him as he lifts up Jesus, hold him when the enemy oppresses"

Bill expresses this, "I know that mom is with the Lord. I would not have that change if I could. I myself long to be with the Lord. I guess I have not taken the time to let myself miss mom. I know I do. It was so quick for me. I was talking with her on that Thursday and then get the phone call a couple of days later that she had died. I do not remember how long prior to her death, that I had seen her. I remember her unconditional love for each of us. I know she sacrificed a lot so that her children could

Joel M. Mulholland

have different things. She was of course, a great prayer warrior, like dad. I always enjoyed talking about spiritual things with her and dad and gleaning their insight and knowledge of God."

My son Daniel Benton, My Jewish son, His letters bless our hearts because they are filled with the word of God. "Even now, For him to live is Christ. Christ liveth in him. His song, I'm sure is, "Make me like you Lord. Make me like you. You are a servant, make me one too. Lord I am willing, do what you must do. To make me like you."

"And he is. Loving, caring, faithful and humble like Jesus. Bless and keep O' Jesus!"

Daniel trumpets this: "Sweet hour of prayer! Sweet hour of prayer! May I, thy consolation share, Til, from Mount Pisgah's lofty height, I view my home, and take my flight: This robe of flesh I'll drop and rise, To seize the everlasting prize, And shout, while passing through the air, Fare-well, fare-well, sweet hour of prayer.

"Prayer was a haven and an oasis for mom. There she met with her Master, Savior, and blessed Father; her blessed heavenly Father that raised her from childhood, and met her and her families every need."

Daniel says, "When Joel related to me her grandpa's description of what happened the morning mom died, it brought to my mind the words of that song. Joel told me that mom had come out of the bathroom and made her way over to sit on the edge of her bed. She proceeded to sit on the edge of the bed, but seemingly didn't make it all the way up, slipped off , and slid to the floor. What I believe , is, as the song says: 'This robe of flesh I'll drop and rise.' Mom made it to the edge of the bed, she heard Jesus say, 'It's time my child,' and he lifted her home. And as she rose, her fleshly body slid to the floor just like a robe falling from her shoulders."

"My son Stephen Joel, a rock of strength, my pillar of strength in quiet assurance. A spirit of calm, a blessing of grace. Faithful, true and loving too!"

Steve heralds quietly, "How does a son put into words what his momma means to him? Words are just print. Feelings, if only one could describe the feelings! I'll give it a shot, but it will be woefully inadequate. I would have liked to have been closer to momma, but I never took the time. I will forever regret that. I will tell you though, momma and I had a quiet connection. I guess you would say an unspoken understanding. I think two words will describe it best, strength and anchor. I gave a quiet strength to momma and she supplied me with an anchor and she still does! An anchor to keep me from drifting too far into the insanities of this world. I could look into her soft, gentle eyes and know truth! Momma would smile at me, and we would both start laughing. Momma had a saucy side to her that unfortunately she kept stifled, but when she did let it out, oh the laughs we would share! I miss momma, but I have one memory I will cherish forever. On one of our visits to see them, momma took us to one of her favorite places. A mountain at the fort, where you could drive almost to the top. Now, if you wanted to go any farther you had to park and walk. Well you guessed it, here was this eighty years young lady pulling her fifty-two year old son up the side of this mountain. Clinging to each other and knowing, filling each other with love and admiration, making our way up the side of that mountain. That's my momma, pulling us all up the mountain that life can sometimes be. I miss my momma to be sure, but I know where she is. Momma is right here with each of us. In our children, our grandchildren and in our minds and hearts! Most importantly momma is with Jesus, and I am so thankful and happy for that and that she is my momma!!!!

I too, have felt this silent assurance from my uncle Steve all my life. The one moment I will cherish forever, is the day he walked into the funeral home, after my sister, Jenny, suddenly passed away. My dad, mom and I sat at this huge table in a room, in the funeral home meshing out the financial end of things. It was so sudden and Jenny had nothing financially to handle this. It was the last thing I cared about and I was frustrated. We needed to come up with just a bit more to pay for the down payment. I looked up from the table to the doorway and there was uncle Steve, always in his favorite jeans and t-shirt, standing quietly. He walked over to me and firmly asked in his deep voice, "How much do you need? I will take care of it!" As his momma said about him: "Faithful, true and loving too."

"My daughter Rose Mary, she is persistently "sweet" and kind, loving, childlike. We're bound together in the bundle of life. Courageous, strong and always helpful. She loves Jesus, I know."

Rose expresses this, "When I was about ten years old, mom, Becky, and I walked to Kingston stadium from our house on E avenue (about three miles), for a dog show. We had the most wonderful time. It wasn't just the cooking and cleaning that she did, but the little things. Like helping with girl scouts, going camping and staying in a cabin with us. Even now when I clean out the end tables I find cards and little things fall out of them that she placed in them, such as pressed flowers, just little surprises. I loved the way she brought out all things in nature."

"My daughter Rebecca Ann, she is brave, kind, loving and holds her children in prayer and as a great love for her parents."

Becky reflects on these memories: "Our dad worked eleven to seven and slept during the day. Once in awhile, after he got up, him and mom would take us to Dairy Queen with the little time dad had. We would put the seat down in the back. We didn't have air conditioning on those hot, humid nights, so we would go for rides. They took us to the drive-in, there was a set of swings there and we'd play., Rose, Ben and I."

"Rose and I had to do the dishes, and we would listen to the radio, I can still picture the kitchen, the phone on the wall.

The whole setting with mom there. Mom even had a favorite Beatles song, It was, "We Can Work it Out."

Becky continues, "When we went on vacation, mom would journal everything. We went to Louisiana to see my brother David and went to Florida as well. These vacations were wonderful! When we stopped at Grace land, mom picked up leaves outside, I got that from mom."

"Mom also told us we could do anything we wanted, if we just tried to achieve it. She was a driving force behind her kids. She loved us and told us that she loved us. She was an intelligent woman. She would teach us about everything, Shakespeare, Thoreau etc. I love her with all my heart. She was a light in the world, and the light went out when she died!"

I agree with aunt Becky, I can't help but think of the song, "this little light of Mine. I'm gonna let it shine…". Anyone who went to Sunday school can relate to this one. I can recall grandma singing this with all of us little ones and with such sincerity. She meant it! Of all the scriptures that I have read in the Bible, there is one that defines who she was to all those who really knew her. (Mathew 5:16) Let your light so shine before men, that they may see your good works, and glorify your Father which is in heaven.

"Benjamin Phillip, Son of my right hand. Such confidence and excellence. Somehow allays my anxieties. Is wise in business; faithful and loving to his wife and daughters. He gave his heart to Jesus at age ten, Holy Spirit following. I know, as he prays for his parents."

Benjamin proclaims this of his mom. "Mom meant to me. A loving heart, caring, sharing, sensitive, humble yet proud, fiercely competitive, giving, open, nature lover, people lover, family first, self last, ego builder, loyal, integrity, honest, truthful, positive, creative, well read, dedicated, intelligent, resourceful, healer, excellent cook, decorator, warm home atmosphere, Christmas, birthdays, Halloween, Valentine's day, Thanksgiving, lover of football, especially the Packers! She was a beautiful woman, great grandmother, teacher, preacher, generous, lover of God, faithful, friendship, funny, youthful, school PTA, ice cream socials, college student, a super wife to a great husband, animal lover, playing football with me when no one else would, consistency, disciplined, hard working, respect, Spring, Summer, Fall, Winter, and in one word, "Perfection!"

Ben ends by saying, "Joel, I have stories and memories that match every thought that I have listed about Mom, but then I would have to write my own book. What a woman! The only comforting thought is that we will all get to see her again in the future. I'm sure she is having a great time in heaven and holds a premiere seat. She has the reward she worked for all of her life."

Grandma finishes her thoughts with this: "So Joel, "They that wait upon the Lord, shall renew their strength." (Isaiah 40:31) "Keep your sons in prayer before the Lord! He hears and answers according to his will. Love from your grandma in Jesus."

A few years after grandma passed away, my grandfather called me. "Hellooo" he says in his strong, deep voice, "I have found something you might like to add to your story. A few weeks after your grandma passed away, I received a poem from my nephew, Doug Long. Let me read it to you. As he read it to me, I thought, wow! People were really observant of this couple. Every testimony of them and of grandma has just about the same content, accept, in their own words. So here's how it goes;

Mr. Bear Hug And Little Lady

Mr. Bear hug and little lady, oh they were a pair!
For almost 63 years, they did share
Who both loved the Lord with all their heart
They were together "Till death do us part"
We are sad, but glad that Darlene is not here
Though yet gone, she is in heaven and always near

Her love for Jesus and us, was always there
She was always loving, kind and fair
Now Mr. Bear is not ready to go
He's got many things to do, you know
He's not sure yet on what they are
But God knows, Who's always near and never far
What did the little lady always have to say?
That Jesus and love are the only way
Yes, Gerald is my uncle, is he
And Darlene, my aunt was she.

And so the next generation blossoms, children grand as grandpa would say. Each of us received her love as it was needed, as she prepared us for life. She instilled the faith of our Lord and knowledge into each who would receive it. Drowning us with compassion in her voice and in her eyes, so genuine. Knowing, sensing our needs, setting aside her own to soothe and bring peace to our own lives, never holding back the truth we needed to hear whether we liked it or not. She did it, and she did it very well! She knew when she was right and never backed down when it came to the truth! She was a great believer in closeness of family and worked to keep us all as close as possible.

Grandma loved each grandchild in the way each needed and she held every one of us very special before Jesus. Each of us hold something precious that she gave from her heart.

Knowing how much family meant to grandma, cousin Cindy Mae, in August of 2005, passed on this message to the family: "Grandma was the glue that held the family together, and now that she is gone, it is up to us as a whole family to keep that "glue" binding. All of us are the glue that keeps the family together."

Three months after grandma passed away I received a card from my cousin Sara Jean. She writes to me, "I'm struggling over grandma as well. Sometimes the strangest things make me think of her. Sometimes when I'm outside with the kids and the wind blows gently on my face, I think she's watching over me, watching over all of us."

Her grandson Jered Jubal tenderly writes this after grandma passed away, "Grandma very much reminded me of flowers. So very grand in beauties essence; poise, strengthened in light; arrayed with the utmost of kindness; the very meaning of heart. I never know if people hold things the way I do. I know that Grandma held flowers as I do; I knew she held my heart and was the only lady to never let it go!" "I'll never forget how she smelled of lavender and always spoke my name with love when I entered her home. How every single time I came to her house she was always there."

And then there were the great grandchildren. Oh how the number began to grow, and each one received a portion of her love, if only for a short time. My son Colin at age 14 revealed his thoughts on his great grandmother, and I am ever thankful that each of my children felt her encouragement and strength. Colin writes, "What can I say. There's a lot of good things I can remember about her. I remember going over to her house, and she always had a smile on her face for me. Her expression was a golden one. She had a great way with children. I guess that came from lots of experience! She was always at church. She was inspired and lifted by the Lord. She was a great listener. When I found out they were moving to Arizona I cried all the way home, but then later she sent me letters, and I would write her back. It was about eight in the morning when I found she passed away, I remember. I think of her almost all the time, and I hope to see her in Heaven some day."

My oldest son Daniel, who is now pursuing writing in college, honestly writes with a conscience;

"When I think of my great grandmother, many things come to my mind. The frosted oatmeal cookies she always had sitting on her kitchen counter, open for anyone who wanted one, to freely take. The warmth of her home in the winter, eating popcorn while watching one of our many Disney movies. Various members of the family stopping by, many of whom I didn't know or remember as though her house was the official meeting spot. I also remember her dog , Gidget. One of the nicest dogs I ever met, and it was that very dog of hers that gave me a memory that I remember to this day, and always will. A lesson of sorts.

"It was in the afternoon, and I was sitting with my grandpa, eating pizza. Gidget was in the kitchen with us and went over to my grandpa, begging for some pepperoni. When my grandpa wouldn't give her, me being the young kid I was, I asked why she couldn't have any. Grandpa answered and said, "Because it's bad for her and it will hurt her stomach.

"I looked from my grandpa to Gidget, who was now on my side of the table, looking up at me with longing in her eyes. Feeling sorry for her, I slipped a couple of pepperonis to her when grandpa wasn't looking. Gidget seemed so happy, I almost wondered if my grandpa had been joking when he said it could hurt her.

"Awhile later, it could've been weeks, it could've been months, it was so long ago, my great grandmother came up to me. She said something was wrong with Gidget and she was in a lot of pain, so they were going to have to put her to sleep. My heart sank down to my feet, as I thought about my grandfather's warning and how I didn't listen. I never told her I thought it was my fault and I wish I had.

"Something about my great grandmother, Darlene, that I liked was, within her Christianity , she let people be themselves. One time I told her the storyline about my favorite television show, a show that happened to be a little violent. The thing I respected about her was, despite her Christianity , she listened to me and added her two cents, but in a non-forceful way. She just wanted to make sure I knew right from wrong, and I did."

Whether family or friend, grandma gave of herself from her heart. She had a great impact on most of those she came in contact with.

Her closest and dearest friend for over 30 years knows first hand. This friend is Vivian Lambert. A wonderful, gentle person and a soft spoken soldier for salvation. She has been a wonderful influence to me, and my father at times as well. Vivian lives up on Belmont hill just down from where grandma and grandpa lived for awhile in Cedar Rapids, Iowa. It began with a cup of sugar. Vivian kindly steps back and reveals to me how it all began. I can just hear her speaking gently, slowly, and ever so softly. She writes, "It's Saturday morning, early and still cool. A gentle south breeze is blowing.

"The word! The word! The word, Vivian! Get into the word!! That's what I remember about Darlene Mae Long! That's why I call her "my mentor!" That's why I now praise God for calling her "HOME" now that her work here on this earth is done!

"So thank you, Joel, for phoning me and asking me to write down some of my memories about this friend.

"How did we meet? I was attending a Bible study at Helen Anderson's at 1211 Belmont, when we heard a knock on the door. "Could I borrow a half cup of sugar?" The woman asked.

"Sure." Helen answered. "C'mon in!"

"And when it was noted that a Bible Study was in progress, this new neighbor was interested! A few minutes later, when we'd ended our session, we walked home together. This new neighbor, three houses down the street. And, along that way, she had said to me, "I've been praying for a New Friend, I think you're that one."

"That's how it happened, some thirty or forty years ago.

"Another incident that I love to report, many times I've told it. As mother's (she had seven children and I had four) frequently in summer time, when the weather was nice, we would go to the place we called "the little green cathedral" It was on the edge of "Mr. Rich's woods", at the very dead end of Belmont parkway. A group of trees was there, one with low hanging branches that literally invited the passer-by to "come rest awhile." With Bibles in hand (Darlene never went anywhere without her "God's Word!") we would enter, sit down on a brought- along- blanket, and smile with gratitude for "Such a place as this!" Blackberries grew on a hill a little north of us, and bore luscious fruit in July. Birds were everywhere, noisy J-birds watched for ripening fruit, chortling their thanks to the God who provides such treats. It had rained a little the night before, just enough to encourage the mosquitoes to come forth and bother the two women who'd just intruded, One lit on my arm, I smacked im!!"

"Oooohhh! Vivian! Don't do that! Ask God to bless them and they won't bite you!" Darlene insisted.

"Somehow in that incredibly, believing moment, I did ask him, and they didn't bite me!! Remember how he (God) ordered hornets? How he prepared a worm? And ordered ravens to feed Elijah? Couldn't he tell his mosquitoes not to bite two of his believing little girls, sitting there, under one of his trees?

And so it is that these two fine women will remain friends for eternity. Grandma in heaven and Vivian awaiting her time as well. Vivian says at the end of her last letter to me:

"I miss her, too. Tho' not like most, I know. But praise God there's a "Great getting up in the morning" just over the hilltop. Just think of it Joel!!! No more tears, no more cryin, all because "He lives! He lives!"

Several years ago, Darlene phoned, asking about this song she'd been remembering. I found it, happily, in a Free Methodist booklet that Bessie Wilcox had given me for Christmas in 1987. (Bessie being a loving acquaintance to us all in the church) I'm delighted anew to ponder the words and praise him all over again. Perhaps you would like to share it with all as well.

So I give to you the hymn that truly represents grandma and her love for the Lord.

"My God and I"

My God and I go in the field together,
We walk and talk as good friends should and do;
We clasp our hands, our voices ring with laughter
My God and I walk thru the meadows hue.
He tells me of the years that went before me,
When heavenly plans were made for me to be,
When all was but a dream of dim conception.
To come to life, earth's verdant glory see;
When all was but a dream of dim conception.
To come to life, earth's verdant glory see.
"My God and I will go for aye together,
We'll walk and talk and jest as good friends do;
This earth will pass, and with it common trifles,
But God and I will go unendingly;
This earth will pass, and with it common trifles,
But God and I will go unendingly.

While attending the Free Methodist church in Cedar Rapids, Iowa and through other spiritual encounters grandma grew a garden of true many friends in Christ. Throughout the years she remained a wonderful confidant to them. Among them was Shirley Bear, now residing with her husband, who ministers in the Free Methodist church in Marion, Iowa, a small town on the outskirts of Cedar Rapids. I couldn't possibly leave her out. She happily wrote this about grandma:

Tribute to Darlene Long

"Knowing Darlene, was one of the highlights of what a Christian was and an example of what made you desire to grow in the Lord.

"She always had the well-worn Bible that had been read and underlined over and over. When she would testify during a service she always had the Bible in her hand and spoke directly to the congregation. When she spoke, you listened and wanted to listen. She had a face that radiated Christ's love.

"She was a morning person, I was a night person. One morning I got a phone call from her. I was sound asleep and Darlene said, "Shirley get your Bible." She was excited about some verses, and she wanted to share them with me! So, there I sat in the middle of my bed, trying to wake up and look for the scriptures!

"Then there was the time she lost a brooch that her mother had given her. She asked for prayer, but for years it never showed up, until much later when she came to our church here, and told us that they had been digging up the yard in their former home and found something shiny. Yes, you guessed it. There was her broach. Does prayer work? There's no doubt about it!

"Whenever I loaned Darlene a book, it would come back underlined with notes along the margin. I felt blessed by it because after all, we were sisters in Christ! Lastly, Darlene was a true women of God. She loved God's word and when you saw her, you saw her Bible. She was also a real prayer warrior, in touch with heaven all the time.

"Jesus was truly Darlene's first love and her family was truly her second love. Shirley Bear, Cedar Rapids, Iowa.

Shirley is absolutely right about loaning her books. She couldn't help it. When she read a book she had to bring out the important points and keep notes and this is how she did it. She underlined and wrote in the margins. Her Bibles were full of it. That's why I so love to read and look through them. Not only for the points, but she also kept little sayings and heart felt needs there along with defining meanings of the scripture or line of a book.

Before leaving Cedar Rapids to live in Arizona, grandma and grandpa were attending Redemption Missionary Baptist Church. They attended for several years and touched many lives along the way. Evangelist Frances White attending in this congregation gives her thought on grandma. "I evangelist

Joel M. Mulholland

White would just like to say this about mother Long. She was a women of integrity, full of wisdom, and loved people. She was willing to help in every way she could. She inspired so much when she taught Sunday school class and gave her testimonies. I am happy to have known her. She is missed at Redemption."

I haven't covered even a fourth of the people she touched. She gave the gift of herself to everyone and without resistance blessed and prayed for them in the way they needed. She felt a personal responsibility to make known the Word of God and to help meet the needs of those around her. This could not be without the true knowing of Christ, and walking in the Word of God without selfishness!

Chapter 10
Eternity (John 3:16 For God so loved the world that he gave his only begotten son, that whosoever believeth in him should not perish, but have everlasting life.)

In most books there is a conclusion. I looked up the word in the dictionary. I found, conclusion: the last part of something, result, outcome. An act or instance of concluding. To complete, bring to an end, finish. This doesn't fit, for this is not the end of my grandmother's faithful journey.

I choose to call this last chapter eternity. Again, I went to my dictionary and looked up eternal. I couldn't believe it. It said: having infinite duration, everlasting. Characterized by abiding fellowship with God. (good teacher, what must I do to inherit life?-Mark 10:17) Not only did the dictionary have Mark ten listed and quoted it, but I had already pulled the scripture of Matthew 19:16-17 from the Bible to put in this portion, not knowing what the dictionary would reveal for a definition: And behold one came and said unto him, Good Master, what good thing shall I do, that I may have eternal life? And he said unto him, Why callest thou me good? There is none good but one, that is, God: but if thou wilt enter into life, keep the commandments. I see this verse as grandma's fulfillment. Her works, she finished, as unto the Lord, fulfilling her personal responsibility to those she came in contact with and kept the commandments. She is now in the presence of Jesus. We can't be with her, but if we work to keep the commandments choose to be born again, we too, shall have everlasting life.

As I sit here this January day and watch the snow come down, I reflect on grandma's thoughts of snow. For everything, she gave me scripture. (Job 37:5-6) God thundered marvelously with his voice; great things doeth he, which we cannot comprehend. For he saith to the snow, Be thou on the earth; likewise to the small rain, and to the great rain of his strength. Her words echo with this scripture, "It is raining now, softly and tenderly. He is watering the earth, and his Holy Spirit is watering my spirit and heart."

This is how she lives on in me. Always feeding me with her tender words of the heart. I can't forget her. I think of her when the first heavy snow starts to fall, and the warmth of home overwhelms me, when I step out to get the mail in my bare feet on a bitter winters day. I sense her near to me when I wipe the tears from my children's eyes, when I hear a cardinal chirp or see a dove land on my bird bath. The breath taking beauty of nature or the first days of a new season. Everyday I look out upon the earth and say, "Where is she today in the spirit of Christ, to remind me?" With the birds, in a song, in a beautiful rainbow, or perhaps in the scent of a breeze upon a lilac bush? I sense her when I flip the tissue-like pages in my Bible. That sound resounds in my conscience, that I should keep myself disciplined to read it and believe it.

Grandma taught me that all the hardships I have gone through in Christ are more rewarding than if I had never experienced any struggle without Christ. Everyone who knew grandma knew she was a great prayer warrior. She emphasized staying in prayer. Then moving on and leaving it as some say, "In God's mailbox." Then waiting on the Lord. The answer will come.

She said to me once, " Need help Joel? Look up and rebuke the enemy! All your needs will be fulfilled. Stay in the Word! Don't ever do anything without faith in Jesus Christ."

This is ma grandmere.